"I want you, Maggy," Joshua murmured softly, rubbing his fingers up and down the softness of her neck.

Moving the waves of her hair aside, he cupped the back of her head in his hands and held her still while he pressed his lips to hers with fierce, passionate need.

"Joshua," she gasped, barely able to speak as his mouth left a trail of sizzling kisses along her throat and collarbone. She curled her fingers in his hair, moaning softly as he nibbled along her neck. "Please, Joshua—"

"That's my intention . . . to please . . . you." Pulling her close to his chest, he slipped the strap of her teddy down, branding the delicate skin of her shoulder with his heated embrace."

"Oh, Joshua, what are you trying to do to me?" she said softly.

"Playing doctor, like I promised." He brushed his lips tenderly across the pale swelling of her breasts. "Now, Maggy," he pleaded, moving his mouth even lower, "let me listen to your heart . . ."

WHAT ARE *LOVESWEPT* ROMANCES?

They are stories of true romance and touching emotion. We believe those two very important ingredients are constants in our highly sensual and very believable stories in the *LOVESWEPT* line. Our goal is to give you, the reader, stories of consistently high quality that may sometimes make you laugh, sometimes make you cry, but are always fresh and creative and contain many delightful surprises within their pages.

Most romance fans read an enormous number of books. Those they truly love, they keep. Others may be traded with friends and soon forgotten. We hope that each *LOVESWEPT* romance will be a treasure—a "keeper." We will always try to publish

LOVE STORIES YOU'LL NEVER FORGET
BY AUTHORS YOU'LL ALWAYS REMEMBER

The Editors

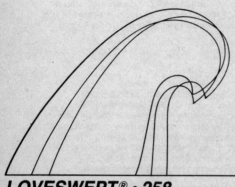

LOVESWEPT® • 258

Margie McDonnell
Conflict of Interest

BANTAM BOOKS
TORONTO • NEW YORK • LONDON • SYDNEY • AUCKLAND

CONFLICT OF INTEREST

A Bantam Book / June 1988

LOVESWEPT® *and the wave device are registered
trademarks of Bantam Books, a division of Bantam
Doubleday Dell Publishing Group, Inc. Registered in U.S.
Patent and Trademark Office and elsewhere.*

*If you would be interested in receiving protective vinyl
covers for your Loveswept books, please write to this address
for information:*

> *Loveswept
> Bantam Books
> P.O. Box 985
> Hicksville, NY 11802*

ISBN 0-553-21679-1

Published simultaneously in the United States and Canada

---

*Bantam Books are published by Bantam Books, a division
of Bantam Doubleday Dell Publishing Group, Inc. Its trademark, consisting of the words "Bantam Books" and the
portrayal of a rooster, is Registered in U.S. Patent and
Trademark Office and in other countries. Marca Registrada.
Bantam Books, 666 Fifth Avenue, New York, New York 10103.*

PRINTED IN THE UNITED STATES OF AMERICA

O   0 9 8 7 6 5 4 3 2 1

One

"Ms. Dailey, I think you'd best move to the center of the raft now and hold tight. Things are going to get even rougher from here on. The Colorado in winter ain't nothing like the Colorado in summer, you know, even here in Arizona."

No. She hadn't known. But she did now. Magdelena Dailey turned seasick green eyes up toward her grim-faced river pilot and wished, not for the first time today, that he had been as honest about their safety as he had been interested in getting paid. Or that for once, just *once*, she'd listened when the other local guides told her she was crazy to make the last leg of her trip to Whitewater Lodge via raft.

She moaned in stomach-churning misery. Why had she succumbed to burritos with *everything* for lunch? After a few humiliating moments with her head over the side, Maggy removed her life jacket to clean it in the rushing water, then speedily donned it again. She was used to gliding along on calm, shallow lakes, never anything like the Colorado River, which wasn't ever really placid. How she could have imagined this "excursion" would be fun was, at the moment, beyond her comprehension.

"Oh, good lord, here we go again!" Squeezing her eyes shut in a childlike effort to make the nightmare go away, she clung to the side of the raft and rode out a comparatively minor set of white water rapids.

"Are we over the worst of it yet?" she asked plaintively, her eyes still closed in the hope that if she couldn't see the whirling water, her stomach wouldn't notice it.

"Not even hardly," the pilot said as their craft was yet again flung from one side of the river to the other.

Not even hardly? "Damn you, Wes Dailey!" Magdelena cursed her ex-husband between clenched teeth, glad that a sudden patch of rapids and their accompanying roar prevented her companion from hearing her. "If I get off this river alive, I swear I'm going to—" She stopped speaking and took a series of long, deep breaths to keep from getting sick again, too preoccupied to think of any retribution horrible enough to wish on her former husband. It was *his* fault she was here in the first place. The rat!

A real estate broker with an eye for "hot properties," Wesley James Dailey hadn't told her that he was into "multiple listings," so to speak, until after she'd been working in his office as a real estate agent for a year and a half—not until after they'd been married for a year, though she'd had her suspicions before. Thus when he'd come to her asking for a quick out-of-the-country divorce in order to court a widow with a huge tract of land in downtown Chicago, it hadn't come as a complete surprise. Which wasn't to say it hadn't hurt. It had; admittedly, mostly her pride. And it didn't soothe her battered ego one little bit to know that he'd given her Whitewater Lodge, his soon-to-boom investment property, as an inducement for cooperation on her part. Still, she'd accepted it. She had to get away from Chicago. She needed an income now that working for Wes was no longer an option. What she hadn't expected was a registered letter informing her that if back taxes on the property weren't paid immediately Whitewater Lodge and its river-rafting charter service would be auctioned off to pay them. She'd sent the check—even though it meant cleaning out her savings account, even though it meant moving to Arizona and taking up the reins of business right away. And she'd decided it meant understanding every little thing about the business. So, after all, if one expected customers to pay for a ride down the river, it seemed a good idea to know what the ride was like. Now it no longer seemed such a good idea. In fact, the more she thought about it, the more she believed it rivaled her marriage to Wes as one of her less intelligent ideas.

The shoreline, only a few yards away, was streaking by with lightning speed. It was obscured from view for long intervals as the raft was swallowed by deep troughs of river water.

Magdelena kept her eyes trained on that elusive shoreline as much as possible, ignoring the stinging spray of water in her eyes, as if the permanence of the land itself could somehow lend her own precarious position some stability. Trees, rocks, bushes; a beach there, a sandbar over here. She looked for places to swim for if, perish the thought, they capsized. But if they were going to have to go swimming, she wanted to be prepared.

As if on cue the boat heaved and twisted, threatening to turn broadside into the waves, its edges tilting dangerously upward as the pilot fought for control. Where was she going to swim to? She searched the shore with a greater sense of urgency, catching sight of a solitary figure standing down-stream, waving his arms wildly, as the raft headed into another series of swirling, swallowing rapids. He obviously wanted to communicate something to them, but his message wasn't coming across.

Maggy was long past ready to listen to any voice of reason. She was ready to walk to the lodge rather than face another half hour in this tub! She turned to the pilot to tell him what she'd decided, and to ask him where the nearest drop-off point might be. But the question never left her mouth. The raft was sucked into the largest white water rapids she'd seen so far, and there was nothing to do but hold on for dear life as an enormous wave lifted them up. From their height on the water she could see the man standing on an outcropping of rock, no longer waving his arms to get their attention. Why had he stopped?

She knew the answer as soon as their watery roller-coaster ride took a sudden change in direction, drop-ping them with all the speed of Superman outrunning a speeding bullet, down into a foaming, frothing maelstrom of white water and sharp-edged rocks. The immediate sound of rubber tearing and ice-cold water splashing over her head prevented any further speculation about how and where she might get to shore. She'd get to shore, all right, Maggy thought desperately, in little itsy-bitsy pieces scattered here and there and everywhere. Fish bait. No, she de-cided as she was swept into the river, she was most definitely not going to recommend this raft trip to her customers, not without paid-up accident insur-ance.

"Don't panic, Red! I'll get you!"

Get her? Magdelena could hear the deep, booming male voice even over the roar of the river, and though she couldn't have had any way of being sure, she knew that it belonged to him, the man who'd had the good sense to travel overland. She turned and tumbled in the water like a redheaded rag doll, unable to see him or the land or anything except the freezing gray water around her. Get her? Fat chance. If she couldn't see him, she had no idea how he was going to see her, much less pluck her from a watery grave. Nonetheless, she held out a small hope that he would get her, and soon.

She'd only been in the water for a minute, but she was already shocked by the cold and battered by the rocks. She knew her arms and legs would be covered with scrapes and bruises. Even though she was wearing a life jacket, she felt at the mercy of the river's force. She'd been doing her best to dog-paddle, but it was a losing battle. Her muscles were all but exhausted with the effort and just a couple of minutes had passed now. Fighting her fear and the force of the current, she listened, almost sure she'd heard the man's voice again. But before she could locate it, the river had swept her along, away from anything she might hope to cling to for support, away from him, wherever he might be. She held her breath and closed her eyes, trying to protect her head with her hands as the river sucked her under the surface and dragged her through yet another series of rapids, battering her against its maze of partially submerged boulders. She surfaced and gasped for air. Somewhere in the back of her mind that small voice of reason was telling her to stay calm. As a sharp stick stabbed into her side, she cried out in a croak that was none too calm, the sound garbled and strangled by a mouthful of water.

She fought against losing consciousness. She had to stand! She had to find a way to keep her head above the water or she was going to drown. She couldn't afford to drown! There wasn't enough money left in her checking account to pay for a decent burial. She quelled her fears, both the rational and the ludicrous, and finding her feet, tried to plant them firmly on the river bottom. But the current was too strong, pulling her feet out from under her again and again. She tumbled out of control, the fear and panic she'd been working to avoid rising up and taking over. Her carelessly tied life jacket had been dragged off by the current. She flailed about in terror, trying to hold onto anything, catch anything that would stop her mad flight downstream with the river.

"Don't try to stand!"

She could hear his voice, a calming influence, much closer this time.

"Stay on your back and point your feet downstream so you can see where you're headed. When you see my shirt, grab hold of it and I'll pull you out of the water."

Listening to the man through that small corner of her mind still responding to reason, she did as she was told, surprised to see him as he came into view just ahead of her. She tried to focus on him, blinked a few times, then realized she'd lost both of her contact lenses. Still, she could see that he had used the rocks as giant stepping stones and come out from the shore as far as he could. Even now he was precariously balanced between water and sky. Wearing only the bottoms of a white jogging suit, he extended the sweatshirt top, holding it tightly in one hand, letting the end trail in the water. Straining to get closer, he gripped the rock with his bare toes and leaned out a little farther.

As the river brought her ever closer, her gaze never left him or the slim hope he held out to her. If anyone could rescue her, she told herself, he could. In any case, he was her last hope. Further ahead the river was squeezed into a narrow corridor of steep rock walls that would provide no landfall.

As she neared, she reached out for him, using all the reserves of strength left to her. But at the last second the river swirled his shirt out of her grasp, and she did nothing more than graze it with the tips of her fingers as she swept by. Their gazes caught and held in mutual anguish as she rolled over and tried to swim back to him. It was an exercise in futility. The river had won. Her fate was no longer in his hands. He had done everything he could do to rescue her, everything a sane man would do to help her. He had done his best. It just hadn't been enough.

Magdelena turned for one last look at him, then her eyes widened in disbelief. The luck of the Irish was with her today. She'd been blessed with an *insane* man. He'd stripped off his jogging suit pants and, clad in nothing more than a pair of nylon running shorts, he dove like a seal into the water, racing toward her. She blinked and was torn between trying to focus on the hit-and-run rocks that seemed to be going out of their way to crash into her, or on the man who'd swan-dived into the frigid water as unhesitatingly as if it had been his own backyard pool.

"I've almost got you, Red. Hold on," a labored voice behind her shouted.

Magdelena heard his voice and felt his presence in the same instant. He wrapped his hands in her long hair and pulled himself alongside her. Holding her close, he kept one hand wound tightly in her hair and used the other to capture her flailing arms.

"Don't fight me!" he yelled into her ear. "I know you're not Rapunzel, but you're no mermaid either, even if you do look like one with all this hair, so for Pete's sake, don't fight me. Trust me and I'll get you to shore!" Using one arm to pin her tightly to his body, he undulated his hips against hers and pressed his thighs this way and that to force her to mimic his movements, using their bodies as a rudder. He steered for a gargantuan boulder regally holding court in the middle of the river.

At the last instant before contact, Magdelena found her head crushed against her rescuer's large, well-muscled chest, safeguarded from the rocks. Her shoulders were pinned, her back supported by his widely splayed hands. Even so, when they hit the pebbled gray surface of the boulder and slithered around to the downstream side, it was like running into a brick wall at full throttle. It knocked the breath out of her and the world turned dark and dizzy for a moment.

"Red! Red, don't even think of passing out on me now!" Treading water for them both, he yanked on a handful of her hair, forcing her to respond.

She gasped for breath, her lungs trying to make up for the moments when she hadn't been breathing at all. Her pulse was beating quickly and erratically and a layer of goose bumps covered her skin. She was aware of a reaction to the fear and the freezing water, and the shock of being slammed against a two-ton rock. Could it also be a reaction to the man himself? she wondered. To this brave man, obviously strong, whose long, sinewy legs were trying to tread water and wrap themselves around her at the same time? Or to Herculean arms that were keeping them both afloat? What would have happened to her if he hadn't come to her rescue? She mewed a small, anxious sound and did her best to swim on her own.

"My name isn't Red," she corrected him breathlessly, her eyes wide and vulnerable as she looked up at him. "It's Magdelena, like in the Bible . . . sort of." Suddenly she realized she wasn't thinking straight—the frigid water, the danger, the nearness of this stranger threw all of her thought processes into disorder.

"Well, then, Magdelena-like-in-the-Bible-sort-of, do you mind telling me just what you were doing rafting down the winter Colorado without a life jacket on?" He raised his voice to be heard above the water. "Did it ever occur to you what a stupid thing to do that was—your so-called 'guide' should have his license revoked for agreeing to take you!" He was yelling at her with as much relief as anger, his hands gripping her body all the tighter.

"I didn't have a choice." She refused to rise to his bullying. "This river-rafting business I've inherited was thrust upon me in winter, not summer, and if I'm to open shop and make a profit next summer, I've got to learn the business this winter. And, for your information, I *was* wearing a life jacket when I fell out of the raft."

"You're not wearing it now." He demonstrated the point by rubbing his naked chest sideways against her. When she felt her nipples tauten to firm points, she told herself it was the cold, and she wasn't going to listen to any snickering inner voice that whispered otherwise.

She tried to pull back from his tight grasp, uncomfortable with the intimacy of the contact. "If you must know," she said quietly, "I'd taken my life jacket off because I threw up on it, and after I rinsed it off, I didn't refasten the ties very well."

A grin tugged at the corners of his mouth. "That wasn't too sensible."

"About as sensible as jumping willingly into freezing water without a life jacket," she retorted. "Or clothes. At least I'm not swimming around practically in my altogether." Now why had she felt it necessary to remind them both of the obvious? She groaned inwardly.

"No." His pale blue eyes glittered with interest. "But you soon will be." He pushed her back against the boulder, holding her there with the force of his body, holding himself there by precariously balancing on some smaller rocks at the boulder's base. He tugged insistently at the belt loops of her jeans and played with the laces on her boots with one bare foot. "Your clothes won't keep you warmer, but they will drag you down if you have to swim with them on." He unsnapped her jeans, slid the zipper down, and slowly eased the material over her hips until he felt her stiffen in his arms. "Don't fight me, little mermaid. I've explained why, so off with your clothes and no arguments."

There was an authority about him that demanded compliance, something within her that couldn't say no. She held still, fighting an inner anticipation as he divested her of the confining slacks and soaked boots.

She shuddered in his arms, shocked as she recognized her terror blending with desire for him. She didn't know him, yet she made no move to interfere as he moved to unzip her anorak, then undid the buttons on her sodden shirt. How clever of her, she thought wildly, to have worn her stretchy pink teddy under her wilderness garb—why, it was just like a one-piece swimsuit. But he still held her so close. . . . Swiftly she began to wilt in his arms as he gently drew the jacket and blouse off her arms.

"Maggy!" He barked her name, thinking that her weakening grip on him signaled an impending loss of consciousness. "Talk to me. Tell me about yourself. Do you have a husband and a bunch of kids out there somewhere waiting for you, or parents who'd miss you if you didn't come back? Think of them. Don't give up now or you'll drown us both!"

"I have no intention of drowning myself." She gazed straight at her rescuer, beginning to steady herself in his grasp. "And in answer to your question, I have an aunt who'd miss me, no children, and an ex-husband who doesn't make me suicidal, only murderous."

"Good." He smiled in satisfaction and pulled her closer to him and to the meager protection the giant boulder provided. "Murderous people want to live, if for nothing more than revenge. Tell me about your ex-husband."

"You wouldn't be interested." She clamped her lips over chattering teeth, unwilling to reveal herself further to this stranger.

"On the contrary. I'm a captive audience until my friend who saw me go in after you returns with his boat. Besides, I'd like to know what red-blooded American male would have let you get away. If you were mine I'd chain you to the bed before giving you a divorce."

Magdelena peered up at his face, wishing again that she hadn't lost her contact lenses. It was hard enough to see his expression now that dusk was settling over the river, turning everything a deep purple hue, without having to contend with a certain degree of nearsightedness as well. Still, his expression seemed to be sincere, and intense, and a great deal more attractive than she wished it was. . . .

"Don't stare at me like that, Maggy." He tucked her head under his chin and massaged her shoulders comfortingly. "We aren't in any position for me to ravage you, and anyway, I've never had to resort to chaining my women to my bed in order to keep them there."

She believed him, though why he thought that

knowledge would comfort her she didn't know. On close inspection, which was the only kind of inspection she could give him under the circumstances, he exuded masculinity. His tall body was hard and strong enough to cling to for safety, his deep, gravelly voice confident and sensitive enough to soothe her very real fears, his arms protectively tender around her waist. And she knew he was brave. Heaven help a woman if he was a handsome devil on top of all that. He'd be lucky if his women didn't chain *him* to *their* beds. She had to struggle to banish the provocative image of him lying naked on a hand-made velvet quilt, chained to a familiar brass bed. What was she thinking of?

She trembled with the knowledge. She wanted him. They were in the middle of a freezing river with no obvious way to get ashore, with no certainty that they would ever walk on terra firma again, either of them, and she had *that* on her mind? Good girl, Maggy, she thought wryly.

"Maggy . . ." He'd noted her glazed eyes and confused expression. "Are you all right?"

"I, uh, I feel—" She couldn't admit to what she was feeling, not in a million years, not to him, not with him so close to her, his hips hard and inviting against her. "You ought to know how I feel," she hedged. "You're the one who insisted on packing us like a couple of sardines."

He chuckled. "Well, I don't know about you, but I'd feel a lot better if I was a lot warmer, and I don't think we should stick around here freezing our buns off to wait for my friend to show up. Something must have happened."

Sure it had, she thought. To his powers of reason. "We can't call a taxi from here." She sputtered as water was sprayed into her face. "So what do you propose we do?" She looked around from their tenuous position. The shoreline on both sides was sheer rock, rising up the height of several stories of a building.

"We're going to have to swim downstream until we find another landing. We can't just wait for a boat."

"Why not?" she shouted. Other than the fact that she was no longer sure *he* had both oars in the water, waiting for a boat seemed far more sensible than swimming for shore without one.

"Don't argue with me, Red," he said. "We're going on three. One, two—"

"Stop! I can't do that."

"Yes, you can." He tightened his grip on her hair. "Because if you don't swim for it now, you'll be much too cold, too exhausted to do it later, and you'll never make it to shore, especially in the dark." He wasn't attempting to make light of their situation any longer. "You're going to swim for it now, Magdelena, and you're going to make it to shore with me if I have to tie you to my back and swim you there myself!"

"You might have to," she snapped back at him. "My jeans weren't the only thing hindering my swimming before, mister. I've also lost my contact lenses and I'll be lucky if I can *see* the shore without your hands-on help."

"Don't worry," he promised her solemnly, ignoring the fact that she'd just admitted to being as blind as the proverbial bat. "You don't swim with your eyes. You swim with your arms and legs and hands. And in any case I don't plan to take *my* hands off you for some time to come." He flashed her a wide, appealing smile. "I'll get you there by braille if I have to. The way I look at it, you've missed out on some of the best things life has to offer and it has just become my destiny to make sure you experience some of them."

"Life's best experiences?" Her brains cells must be waterlogged and beginning to freeze, she thought.

"Yeah. One of the best of which is me." Drawing her closer, he planted a firm, promising kiss on her parted-with-surprise lips before pushing her off the rock and into the swirling tide. "Now swim! I'm right behind you."

Two

Time lost its usual meaning as they battled their way downriver, fighting the quickly changing current and the increasing darkness. He stayed with her, swimming right beside her, pulling her with him when she faltered, urging her on when she cried out in frustrated defeat, unable to find a landing spot in the cliffs on either side.

"Here. Over here." He guided her to a small sandbar that jutted out from a brushy shore.

"We made it, Red. We really made it," he crooned as they dragged themselves up and away from the swirling water, speaking to her softly as his hands assured him that she was all right.

"I didn't think we were going to make it to the shore," she gasped. Her entire body was shaking with exhaustion and relief and cold, and she instinctively sought the sanctuary of his arms.

"I'll admit to having a few niggling doubts myself, especially when I saw you searching the cliffs with your hands for someplace to land."

"Braille." She sniffed into his bare chest, surprised

to find that some of the water dripping from him came from her own tears. Strange. She hadn't cried when Wes left, but here, in the arms of a stranger, she couldn't seem to stop.

"Hey, hey, Magdelena? Are you hurt?" He quickly examined her body, stroking and touching all of it. "We made it to land. We're going to be all right. Truly. Here." He picked up a handful of wet sand and pressed it into her palm, their fingers meeting, the touch electric, the current flowing between them as strong as the one they'd just left behind. "If you don't believe me, feel this."

She dropped the sand and held his hand up for inspection. The skin was cut and scraped where he'd sacrificed it, instead of her flesh, to the boulder's abrasive surface. Lifting it to her lips, she kissed the hand gratefully, trying not to drop salty tears into the cuts.

"Lord, don't cry," he whispered hoarsely, licking his lips, his eyes heavy with concern and frustration as they locked with hers. "Tell me what it is. Please. I don't want to see you hurt. I want . . ." His face held a wealth of meaning as the knowledge of what he did want surfaced to a conscious level. He let his gaze sweep over Maggy, and he was filled with a fierce need to hold and protect her, to make her his.

Reaching out hesitantly, he lightly traced a line from her bare shoulder down the curving side of her ribs and waist to a dark bruised spot on her hip. "Does it hurt very much?" he asked contritely as she sucked in a ragged breath.

"Only a little," she murmured, her body shaking with a combination of cold and a recognition of how close she'd come to dying. Her shivers increased in intensity, and he pulled her into the warmth of his strong arms.

Had human contact ever been as comforting? Maggy wondered.

He gently pushed back the strands of dark red hair that had fallen into her face, then kissed her forehead. His lips brushed the wet curls on his way down the side of her face, his mouth seeking, searching, yearning.

She lifted her lips to meet him halfway in impassioned, surprised response. She felt a heat begin to flow in her veins, and pressed even closer to this man who touched her lips with such intensity she was transported to a fantasy of steamy warmth and comfort. Was her response partly gratitude? As his generous mouth descended to hers once more, Maggy felt herself respond with equal passion. She'd been unwilling to share this feeling with anyone for so long. This was somehow new, as if she'd held something of herself in reserve until today, in unknown anticipation of him. Destiny? she asked herself. And as if in answer she raised her mouth to meet his. Their breaths mingled, her lips soft and pliant, trusting.

His tongue swiftly, surely, parted her lips, as though he too could sense the need that had overtaken her, and as if he too had been swept away by an exquisite urgency. He ran his tongue lightly over the smooth surface of her teeth before plunging on to taste the sweetness of her inner mouth, warm and mobile and responsive.

Her bruises and cuts were forgotten altogether. Her nerve endings were crowded with too many wondrous sensations to allow discomfort to intrude. The wet sand underneath her could as easily have been a feather bed or a bed of nails, and she disregarded the damp chill in the air as a rising inner heat took over.

Shivers tingled up and down her spine as his tongue left off playing with hers and started a moist, sensual journey down the slender length of her neck, in search of other treasures. Flicking quickly here and there, it left small circles of fire from her mouth to her throat to her slender shoulders and beyond. Her skin flushed with heat as his hands found pleasures of their own, and she lifted her arms to encircle his neck.

"Are you still freezing?" He stopped, half dazed, moving his hands fluidly over her bare arms, feeling the tiny prickles of response dotting her skin.

"Cold," she murmured, snuggling closer to him. "But better . . ." Her voice trailed off.

Levering himself up on one elbow, he brought his mouth back to hers, drinking in the sweet abandon with which she returned his kiss.

"I don't even know your name," she murmured when their lips parted. She shook her hair back and gazed at him in awe.

"It's Joshua." He licked his upper lip. "Joshua Wade. Say it," he ordered with curious intensity. "I want to hear you say it."

"Joshua." Had a mere name ever sounded so sensual?

A faint echo of the word, as if on cue, reverberated in the distance, garbled by the crash of water on the rocks around them.

"Joshuaaaaaaaa. Joshuaaaaaaaaaa!" The voice sounded nearer with each call.

Joshua left her warm arms like a man awaking from a drugged sleep, shaking his head as if to clear it.

"Here!" he yelled in response to the unseen person. "We're over here!" He stood with legs braced wide, looking upriver, one hand still absently brushing her shoulder.

"It's my friend, the one with the boat. I recognize his voice," he explained. When she didn't answer he looked at her, only then aware of the change in her.

Curled up on the sand as far away from him as possible, she was covering her near nakedness awkwardly, an embarrassed frown replacing the previously enraptured expression on her face. She was shivering with the cold, aware of it once again, and took another look at the man she had been embracing. Who was he? And how had he managed to penetrate her defenses so quickly? she wondered as a high-powered motorboat appeared around a bend in the river.

As it zigzagged its way through the same rapids they had recently crossed, she could hear the engine whine as it worked to keep itself on course. The boat's yellow spotlight bobbed and weaved, up and down and around crazily.

Magdelena drew her hair around her shoulders in a quick effort to cover herself as the spotlight finally caught them in its beam. She suddenly felt shy, so revealed before this stranger in her soaked teddy, this man she'd only just met.

"Trust me, Maggy." Joshua caught her hand and brought it to his mouth to brush her fingers with his lips. "Trust your instincts about me," he said, pulling her to her feet and to his side.

"My instincts have proven themselves to be notoriously untrustworthy," she said, curling her toes into the wet sand and trying to look anywhere but into those enticing light blue eyes. "But that doesn't mean I'm not grateful to you. I am. I want you to know that, now, just in case I don't see you again."

"You'll be seeing me again," he promised as the rescue boat landed at their sandbar, its engine shut down to an idle. "We're going to be seeing a lot of each other," he added.

The man in the boat coughed discreetly. "You're already seeing a lot of each other, if you ask me."

Magdelena tore her gaze from Joshua's and looked at the other man. He was middle-aged, wearing a bright yellow rain slicker, and looking wet and out of sorts. He rummaged around in a waterproof box inside the fiberglass boat and pulled out a couple of dry blankets and a wool jacket.

"Here. Sorry they're a bit ratty." He tossed them to Joshua, who caught them in midair and folded a blanket about Magdelena. Then he lifted her into his arms and carried her to a seat in the back of the boat.

"Now that you mention it, the lady and I could use a change of clothes," Joshua said, "so if you'll just turn this thing around and get us back upriver, I'll owe you one, Bailey," he said, donning Bailey's heavy jacket.

"Me too," Magdelena piped up from under the blanket. She held one hand out in friendship. "I've never been so glad to see a boat in all my life. I was beginning to believe that if you didn't come soon he was going to make me swim back the way we came."

"Sorry for the delay." Bailey nodded in her direction and took the proffered hand for a second before revving the engine and turning the boat around. "I would have been here sooner, but I had to fish her pilot out of the drink," he said to Joshua. "I would've let him wash up on his own, but he wasn't swimming any too good."

"Was he badly hurt?" Magdelena asked. She hoped not, feeling more than a little responsible for the accident. She was the one who'd offered him a premium fee in the first place.

Bailey spat out his answer disdainfully, along with a wad of chewing tobacco. "He's got a busted leg and some bruises, and he ain't never going to pilot that raft down the river again. But he'll live, which in my own opinion is more than he deserves."

Joshua's body tensed next to hers, his hold around her shoulders tightening angrily. "As far as I'm concerned, he'll never pilot *any* raft down this river again. But I'll deal with him later. Right now I want to get Maggy to the boathouse and I want you to drive to the nearest phone to call an ambulance."

"I don't need an ambulance, and the accident wasn't entirely the pilot's fault," she started to explain, only to have her confession cut off with an impatient motion of Bailey's hand.

"Doesn't matter." He spit into the water again. "Wade's the boss, and if he says you're going to the boathouse and I'm going to call an ambulance, then that's what's going to happen."

Oh? Who'd died and left Joshua in charge of *her?* She didn't have time to ask. They were already pulling up alongside a boathouse.

Joshua picked her up and carried her out of the boat, leaving the mooring to his partner.

"What did you do with her pilot?" he asked over his shoulder.

"Put him in my truck before I went out after you. Figured I'd have to transport him myself."

"You won't have to." Joshua pushed the boathouse door open with his foot and carried Maggy inside. "Just call an ambulance from the nearest phone and tell them where you are and where we are."

"Right."

"I don't need to be carried," Magdelena said to Joshua once they were inside, deciding to take charge of her own life again. "And I'm not going to the hospital. For one thing, I feel fine. And for another—"

She stopped, embarrassed to confess the state of her finances. "And for another, I don't have any insurance and I can't afford to pay any outrageous emergency room bills when I need the money for other things." Like living expenses until she could get the lodge back on its feet.

"This is my property, such as it is." Joshua set her down on an ancient couch whose dull avocado color matched the chipped paint on the walls. "I have insurance to cover this kind of thing. Don't worry. We'll just say you had an accident here on the grounds." He took a battered first-aid kit from a wooden shelf and extracted several packages of gauze and a bottle of alcohol.

"Let me see your bruises. I'm good at playing doctor."

She ignored his friendly leering grin. "I'm sure you are. But I'm perfectly capable of doing that for myself." She reached for the bottle as he tore one of the packages of gauze open.

"Of course you're capable." He began dousing the pad with alcohol. "But why should you have to do this when I'm here?"

"I'd rather be self-reliant." And at least two feet away from the temptation he presented, she added silently.

"I'd rather you weren't. I like my women to depend on me."

His women? "Mr. Wade—ouch!" She drew her leg back as the alcohol set it on fire. "I realize I may have given you the wrong impression out there on the river." She winced as he applied another gauze pad. "I was scared out of my wits and I may have expressed my gratitude a bit more than I should have, but—ouch!" She bit her lower lip. He was intentionally trying to make the explanation difficult. "But I went through enough with my ex-husband to last me a lifetime. I'm not about to become 'your woman' or any other man's."

He continued dabbing the alcohol, not answering her, dribbling the cool, stinging liquid on her calves and ankles until he had washed all the river dirt away and administered to the majority of her cuts and scrapes. He then eyed her knees intently.

Redefining their relationship would have to wait, Maggy decided. "You're *not* touching my knees," she informed him, hands warning him away as he started toward the worst injuries, alcohol-soaked pad in hand.

"All right." He gave in with deceptive ease. "I won't touch them."

She lowered her hands slowly. "Thanks." It took only a moment for her guard to slip, and even less time for him to pour the alcohol directly onto her scraped knees, straight from the bottle.

"Dammit, Joshua Wade!" She fairly leaped from the couch, her eyes watering, her fists clenched. "You said you wouldn't touch them."

"And I didn't," he said truthfully. "My hands did not come into contact with your skin at any time."

She sank back down onto the couch and pounded her fist against its side. "Uncle! For mercy's sake, Joshua! Wash it off, will you?"

"I can't. We don't have running water here, not in the boathouse. Of course, if you'd care to hop back into the river . . ."

"Forget it." She groaned in painful resignation. "But no more of that." She eyed the bottle. "Just put it away."

He set the bottle down, just out of her reach. "When I was twelve and I skinned my knees skate-boarding down Suicide Hill, my mother caught me and decided to administer first aid on the spot. She sent my brother after the alcohol and she applied it right there in front of my friends *and* the girl I was trying to impress." He looked at her knees and the long, slim thighs peeking out from under the blanket. "She told me that if I didn't sit still, she was going to have to use the only other cure-all, the only other method of fixing hurts in her possession. I fell for it." He crossed his arms patiently. "I'm going to give you the same choice. Are you going to sit still until I finish with you, or are you going to take my mother's cure-all?"

She considered it. She wasn't going to let him, as he put it, finish with her. If he was given carte blanche, she doubted he'd stop with administering to her knees when there was so much unfinished business elsewhere. But how much worse could his alternative be? Well, it *was* his mother's idea and she'd done it in public. Safe enough.

She glanced at the bottle of alcohol, still half full. "Anything, as long as it doesn't hurt."

"I'm going to hold you to that, Red." He clasped both of her hands and moved them aside. Leaning down, he planted one firm wet kiss on the tender skin just above each scrape on her knee.

Magdelena trembled violently. She was filled with a renewed longing for him, wanting him to continue kissing her there and everywhere until all her pain, physical and emotional, was gone. The sensation of his mouth on her knees started a chain reaction, sending a tingling desire through her entire body. She moved away from his touch, unwilling to pick up where they had left off, to start something she wasn't prepared to finish.

"Your mother kissed your knees in front of all your friends?" she asked. Her voice had taken on a husky low quality which gave evidence of her desire, despite the teasing question.

"Uh-huh." He moved a little higher on her leg, whispering the reply into her flesh. "And not only was it a good cure, but good preventive medicine too. I never did go down Suicide Hill again on a skateboard."

"Is there a message in there somewhere for me?"

"Only insofar as running the Colorado in winter goes." He was suddenly serious, tracing with one finger a line down her thigh to circle the places he had kissed on her knees. "As for swearing off men altogether due to one bad experience, I don't think the same rules apply."

"You don't?" A hard lump had lodged itself in her throat, making her breathing difficult and her voice squeaky.

"No, I don't." His subtle tracings had taken on the quality of a gentle massage.

"You don't think once is enough? You think I need to get hurt more than once to learn a simple lesson?" Oh, how was she supposed to think with him caressing her tender skin?

"No." He considered his words carefully, letting his fingers move in slow motion from freckle to freckle on her slender legs. "But then all men aren't suicide hills. Whereas skateboarding down one, if you'll accept the analogy, might leave you with skinned knees, going down another could just be an exhilarating, breathtaking, delightful experience."

"What are you trying to say?" She cleared her throat. More importantly, she thought, what was he trying to do? He'd stopped fondling her legs and was now petting her fingers, still defensively clutching the blanket.

"I'm saying that I don't want you to go out of my

life when you go out that door. I'm saying that I don't want you to run away from me just because you've had one awful experience. More, I'd say this instant chemistry sizzling between us frightens you."

"Frightens me?" She laughed at the understatement. "It scares the pants off me." Poor choice of words, Magdelena. "I may have to get my knees looked at, but I don't have to get my head examined. The last thing I need right now is an intimate relationship. I came to Arizona to take over my ex-husband's business, to make a living for myself, to get on with my life, not to jump from the frying pan right back into the fire. I came to find myself, not to find someone else."

"Are you through?" He covered her mouth with a gentle hand. "Because you've got your logic all wrong. You didn't find me. I found you, remember? And I'm not foolish enough to let you go . . ."

An ambulance siren sounded in the distance, growing louder as it came closer.

". . . at least I'm not foolish enough to let you leave me without giving you a powerful reason for wanting to come back." Moving the waves of her hair aside, he cupped the back of her head in his hands and held her still while he made good on his promise. His lips were firm on hers as he extracted a response, his touch no longer lightly passive, but passionate and not just a little desperate.

"I want you, Magdelena," he murmured softly, rubbing his fingers up and down the softness of her neck. "And before you leave here"—the sound of the siren died away as the ambulance pulled up to the boathouse and stopped—"I'm going to make you admit that you want me just as much, that you'll give us a chance."

A chance? That she wanted him was nothing he

had left to chance. Wanting him was a sure thing. Admitting she wanted him was another matter. She couldn't have even if she'd wanted to, which she didn't. His tongue was busily overwhelming hers, making it difficult to form the words to tell him anything. And his hands were making short work of any conscious thoughts that might have found their way to her tongue.

"Joshua . . ." She got a word in edgewise, letting him kiss the side of her mouth while she spoke. "The ambulance . . ." She curled her fingers in his hair as his lips left her mouth and moved to the back of her neck, tickling her with his nibbling kisses. "It's here now—the ambulance attendants—"

"They'll think I'm giving you artificial respiration." He lowered the blanket from her shoulders.

"If this is artificial, save me from the real thing. I can only stand so much. Joshua, please."

"That's my intention . . . to please . . . you." Pulling her close to his chest, he slipped the strap of her teddy down, branding the delicate skin of her shoulder with his heated embrace.

"Oh, Joshua," she called softly. "What are you trying to do to me?"

"Just playing doctor, like I promised." He brushed his lips tenderly across the pale swelling of her breasts. "If you'd like I can listen to your heart." He laid his head against her chest.

"Yes, it's beating, but much too fast if you ask me. I diagnose stress. Stress'll make your heart pound. But I have a great idea, Maggy. After they've checked you out at the hospital, I'll bring you back home with me and—"

"The ambulance is ready to transport her now," Bailey interrupted them suddenly, sticking his head in the door and giving Magdelena only seconds to pull the blanket back up around her shoulders.

"Should I tell them to come on in?" Bailey didn't wait for an answer, exiting with as much speed as possible.

"Do you think he noticed anything?" Joshua's question was tinged with amusement.

Magdelena ignored his chuckle and pulled the blanket more tightly around her.

"Is the injured party in here?" a white-uniformed ambulance attendant asked, after knocking on the door and entering the room.

"Yes, I am. But I really don't need to see a doctor. I've got a few bruises and my head aches, but other than that I'll be fine. If I could just ride back to town with the pilot of the boat though, I'd be grateful. He has all my things back at the drop-off point."

"No problem about a ride back, miss." The man escorted her out the door. "But I'd advise you to see the doctor on call anyway. You've been chilled. And you've been bashed around, so you need to have some X rays made. Now, if you'll just come with me, please."

Magdelena climbed gingerly into the back of the ambulance, glancing at her pilot and his makeshift splint.

"We'll need your name, address, and phone number, next of kin, insurance carrier, et cetera," the attendant said, climbing in beside her.

"The rest of that you can get on the way, I'm sure," Joshua said, appearing at the back of the ambulance. "But as for the insurance, have the bill sent to me. The accident happened on my property, and of course I'm insured, but until the insurance company is notified to delete the former owner's name from its records and recognize me as the new owner of Whitewater Lodge, there could be a delay in your payment and I don't want that to happen."

"I appreciate that, Mr. Wade," the attendant said. "So many people nowadays—" He stopped abruptly as Magdelena swayed back and forth, one hand held to her heart. "I think you're right. We'd better get the rest of the information later." He felt for her pulse, jotting down a notation on an information sheet. "This lady looks like she may be going into shock."

"I'm not spending the night," Magdelena informed the burly night nurse who was fluffing her hospital bed pillow with all the finesse of a heavyweight prize fighter. She had been poked and prodded, x-rayed, banded and bandaged, had filled out every form the hospital possessed until she had writer's cramp, and had been asked every question under the sun except the most important one, the only important one as far as she was concerned: Did she intend to stay here? She did not. She had too many unanswered questions that weren't going to be answered from the confines of a hospital room.

"You are if the doctors say you are." The amazon of a nurse moved to bar the door, planting her rubber-soled white oxfords squarely in Magdelena's path of escape. "You can't leave until one of them signs you out."

"I'm signing myself out," Magdelena snapped. "With all the paperwork I've signed, I've probably already signed myself out at least three times. Now, where's Joshua Wade?" She was going to have his hide for doing this to her, and unless he had some pretty good answers, she was going to have his hide anyway. How dare he lie and tell people *he* owned *her* property?

"He went home hours ago after the staff told him

you'd be spending the night, and he won't be back until checkout time tomorrow morning, so there's no way for you to go."

"Wanna bet?" She'd managed to function quite nicely without Joshua Wade for the past twenty-five years. She thought she could manage to check herself out of the hospital without his help now. Pushing her way past the nurse, she held her open-backed hospital gown together and felt her way down the hall, seeing everything in a frustrating fuzziness.

"Excuse me." She stopped what appeared to be an orderly and then realized he was only a man wearing a pair of white coveralls. "I need to make a phone call and I've lost my wallet. Would you be so kind as to lend me a quarter and direct me to the nearest pay phone?"

He regarded her closely. "You aren't from the third-floor west wing, are you?"

"Third-floor west wing?" Did it matter?

"You know, where they keep all the patients with mental problems."

Magdelena counted to ten, hoping the enraged expression on her face didn't label her as an inhabitant, or at the very least a likely candidate for the third-floor west wing. "No," she answered sweetly, "I'm from the second floor, cheap wing. It's hospitalization on the economy plan. No phone in the room, no bedpans, no meals served, nothing. I'm calling my folks to order a take-out hamburger and fries. That is, I will if you'll lend me a quarter."

"Sure, sure." He fumbled in his pocket for change. "Say, what are you in here for?" he asked as he guided her to the nearest phone.

"She's in here for the night." The night nurse caught up with Magdelena just as she dropped the quarter into the slot. "You aren't going to be able to leave here tonight, young lady, phone call or not. Regulations are regulations. So you may as well come back to your room."

"You've read me my rights," Magdelena snapped, her patience wearing terribly thin. "Even someone under arrest is allowed one phone call." She quickly dialed a number. "And this is mine."

"Your attorney?" Her keeper tapped an impatient foot on the polished floor, obviously eager to have this particularly troublesome patient done with for the night.

Magdelena smiled broadly as the ringing stopped and the receiver was lifted on the other end. "Precisely."

Three

"Thanks for springing me." Magdelena smiled gratefully at the woman seated beside her in the sports
car. The woman, who looked like an older version
of Magdelena, was not only an attorney of some
repute, but also Magdelena's only living relative—
sister to her late mother—and her friend. Most of
all, at this moment she was the person who could
straighten out her legal tangle if it needed straightening. "And for bringing my extra pair of contact
lenses."

"You're welcome." The older woman stopped the
car at the exit from the hospital parking lot, vacillat-
ing over which direction to take. "Now, do you mind
telling Aunt Deirdre just where we're going in such
an all-fired hurry, and why I should have spent the
last hour and a half collecting all of your belongings
from a rafting company whose representatives were
begging me not to sue? And do you mind telling me
why I should be listening to your tantrums rather
than the good doctor's advice about where you should
be spending the night?"

"We're going to Whitewater Lodge," Magdelena said firmly. "If possession is nine tenths of the law, then I want to take possession of my nine tenths before somebody else does."

"Pardon?" Deirdre's foot was still on the brake. They weren't going anywhere until she had all the facts.

Magdelena recognized her aunt's formidable court-room manner at once. "Puh-leez!" she begged. "Just make a left turn onto the highway and keep your foot on the accelerator until we're out of town. I'll direct you from there. You can cross-examine me on the way, I promise."

"You're under oath, Magdelena Marie." Deirdre rarely used her niece's middle name, and never un-less she was displeased. "And you don't need to give me directions. I was the one who told your husband—"

"*Ex*-husband, if you please."

"Your ex-husband about Whitewater Lodge. And I live here, Magdelena. I know the streets. You don't need to tell me how to get there, just why we have to, and why we have to do it under cover of darkness."

Magdelena talked nonstop from the hospital all the way to the lodge, glossing over certain events of the day that she thought it wise not to share with her aunt. For in spite of being such a cynical, sharp-tongued, fire-breathing dragon of a woman, Deirdre had on a number of occasions played Cupid in other people's lives, her niece's in particular.

"You shouldn't worry," Deirdre concluded as they ascended the stairway to the main door. "I haven't seen the documents that Wes's attorney drew up yet—"

"Don't start on that again," Magdelena warned, searching in her purse for the duplicate set of keys she'd left there before boarding the raft with the originals. "If I had waited to get the divorce in the

U.S., I'd still be married to Wes, whom, admit it, you never did like, and he wouldn't have handed Whitewater Lodge over to me on a silver platter just for giving him his freedom early. You'd have had to take him to court to get it, a job, I might remind you, that you'd have had to do for me gratis since I don't have any money to speak of and Wes won't have any until after he marries his Chicago land heiress. So there. I've saved us both some time and headaches. Besides, I looked over the document and it seemed simple and straightforward enough to me."

"That's why we're out here in the middle of the night playing Nancy Drew and the Hardy Boys," Deirdre added as the front door creaked open slowly. "Because you're sure you have a legal claim to the place."

"It has nothing to do with legalities. It has to do with too much worry, too little sleep, and acute paranoia. I'll feel better after I see that no one's moved in to claim squatter's rights and set up housekeeping without my permission."

Deirdre flipped the light switch, not expecting the lights to come on. They did, but the scene that greeted them, illuminated by a dusty chandelier, made them both wish the room had remained dark.

Accumulated dust and dirt covered worn carpeting and broken furniture. Cobwebs hung in daring abandon from doorways. And the sound of small skittering feet made both women cringe in disgust.

"I don't think you're going to have to worry about someone else having set up housekeeping here, Magdelena, my love. I'd say our lodge hasn't seen the dust rag of a housekeeper in quite some time."

"I'm going to kill him." Magdelena picked her way across the once lovely front room, kicking a stack of empty flowerpots to one side. "If I have to crawl on my hands and knees all the way back to Chicago,

I'm going to kill Wes. You know, I suspected the lodge might be in financial trouble, but this . . ." She turned around slowly. "This isn't a difficulty. This is a disaster!"

"Look on the bright side." Deirdre rang the desk bell, watching as the dust settled around it and the open register. "Nobody in his right mind would fight you over this. Nobody in his right mind would want it."

"That's not very reassuring." Magdelena grimaced. "I've already met one man today who wasn't in his right mind. Nevertheless, I am looking on the bright side, and I've found one meager silver lining in my dark cloud. Do you want to know what it is?"

"I can hardly wait." Deirdre had the intuition to look skeptical.

"If I recall correctly, you signed a paper at the hospital this evening taking full responsibility if I had a relapse. You *did* promise the good doctors that you'd stick around a few days to help out and see that I didn't overdo." She began climbing the stairs to the second floor, not looking back at her aunt. Her lips twitched in suppressed mirth. Thank heavens for her sense of humor. "Look at things this way, Deirdre. A little time spent helping me out here is better than a breach-of-promise suit, isn't it? Besides, you're always saying that you'd like to take some time off to spend in the country. This way you'll be able to do that and I won't charge you a cent in cash money. You can pay for your room and board in kind. Washing, dusting, scrubbing, painting . . ." The silence behind her was deafening.

"You're not by any chance hinting that *I* should spend one night, let alone several nights here, are you, Magdelena?" Deirdre asked, climbing the stairs after her niece. "And all because I did you the favor of signing your release forms? Do you know what the penalties are for blackmail?"

"Nope." She opened the door to one passable-looking room. "But I know what they are for premeditated murder, and unless you keep me on my chain for a few days, that's exactly what I'm liable to do to Wesley, making you an accessory before the fact." She ducked as Deirdre let fly with a dusty pillow.

"Couldn't I keep an eye on you at the apartment in town?" Deirdre's voice had taken on an appealing, plaintive quality.

"Yes, but then I couldn't keep an eye on Whitewater Lodge."

"Or an eye out for Joshua Wade, hmmm?" Deirdre pulled the covers off the bed, inspecting the sheets for evidence of any four-legged mouse-type inhabitants. "I almost hope he does show up. You've stopped moping and feeling sorry for yourself, you know, and your eyes sparkle every time you mention his name."

"If my eyes sparkle, it's because I'm angry. He said he owns my lodge!" She was suddenly serious. "Aunt Deirdre, if he does show up, then it has to mean that he thinks he has a claim to my property, and that can't happen. I need this place, for lots of reasons, and you have to help me keep it."

"Oh, I will," Deirdre said firmly. "Even if he does put the sparkle in your eyes, the first thing one learns in law school is that the law is sacred, and whether you're getting married for love or lending money to a close friend or financing your brother's house, you get a contract and make it all nice and legal. No matter how fantastic a man he is, or how much I'd like to see you involved with someone decent for a change, unless he has some proof of ownership, he isn't getting his foot in the door."

Maggy reflected on that comforting thought as she and Deirdre remade the beds in the two neatest rooms with some of Maggy's trousseau linens she'd thought to pack. She then donned a soft nightgown and gratefully crawled under the covers. But she couldn't help wishing that Deirdre had waited to reassure her about Joshua Wade. And once Joshua Wade was on her mind, it was difficult to put him aside.

Lying awake twenty minutes later, she stopped counting the cracks in the ceiling and hoping to fall asleep. Under ordinary circumstances, the events of the day would have left her dog-tired, asleep before her head touched the pillow. Why was it that Mr. Joshua Wade seemed to be the exception to the rule when it came to predicting how she would react under normal circumstances? What right did he have to keep her awake, especially when he wasn't here to keep her company? Scratch that. She didn't want him here to keep her company. She wanted to go to sleep. Alone. Dragging the pillow over her head, she resolutely closed her eyes and vowed to dream of anything other than Joshua Wade and the way he made her feel, both good and bad.

Her first conscious thought, an indeterminate amount of time later, was that it hadn't worked. He was there, as big as life, his long masculine body over and under and all around hers. She could feel his lips moving over her face, brushing against her closed eyelids, the end of her nose, her cheeks, the slight cleft in her chin, just as if he were really there. She could smell the fresh male scent of him, a combination of soap, after-shave, and cool river water all rolled into one. It was a little wild, a little untamed, like him, and more than a little unsettling. She could taste that distinctly Joshua taste, recognizable even without sight or sound, as his lips stopped their inventory of her face and found her mouth. She concentrated very hard and tried to banish him again, giving up as his oh-so-real presence interfered with her concentration.

What the heck, it was a dream, right? And while she'd taken a sabbatical from men, it hadn't meant she'd taken one from her fantasies as well. In any case, she wasn't having much success escaping this fantasy. Giving up the battle, she reached out for her dream man, leaving her inhibitions asleep, where they belonged.

His skin was warm, as it hadn't been this afternoon, and she snuggled closer to him, delighting in his warmth, his strength, the very maleness of him that was so different from her. The sparse curling hairs on his legs tickled her tender skin as he rolled over on top of her, but she didn't make any attempt to lessen the contact, the ticklish, exciting feeling transforming itself into something more, transmuted into a delicious desire, more real than any she had ever experienced while fully awake. This desire for him was almost an ache, her need for him no longer something to dream of. She wanted something tangible, something genuine. She didn't want to settle for something imaginary, no matter how vivid her imagination admittedly was.

"I want you, Joshua." She breathed the admission softly into the warmth of his chest. "I want you here with me."

A low chuckle, intimate and very, very close, penetrated the passionate fog she'd seduced herself with. "I *am* here, Red."

She bolted upright in the bed, her large eyes wider than usual, and twice as sparkling as they were when first she went to sleep. It couldn't be. She found herself nose to nose with a completely real Joshua Wade dressed only in snug red pajama bottoms.

"What are you *doing* here?" More to the point, how had he gotten here? He hadn't been hiding under the bed when she went to sleep, had he? She sank back down in dismayed shock.

"I thought I might go to sleep. Or at least that was my intention when I first came to bed." He raised himself to an intimate position, straddling her body, holding his weight off her with his elbows. "But now I don't think I want to go to sleep." He brushed the disheveled hair away from her face, his fingers a healing touch to the forgotten bump on her head. Then he followed the line of her body where it met with his, smoothing the extremely small space between them with his fingers as a potter might do to cracks in a clay vase to cement two halves together.

Magdelena shook her head hard, wondering if the burly night nurse hadn't vengefully drugged her ice water. She was going to try the question again and hope she got better results this time.

"What I meant when I asked what you were doing here was, what are you doing in my bed?" She got no response, as Joshua had begun brushing her throat with tiny kisses.

"Why am I bothering to talk to a dream?" she muttered, trying to ignore the erotic feelings either he or her altered state of consciousness was inflicting on her all-too-willing body. He wasn't there. He wasn't there. He wasn't—he was too! She had to make him stop before she begged him to go on. She pulled his head up by his hair.

"If you're a dream, you're a damned real dream." She attempted to roll out from under him, only to find herself pinned under his legs.

"You are *my* dream, Maggy," he said softly into her ear, licking around its sensitive edges in between compliments. "In *my* home, in *my* bed, and I have no intention of waking up yet . . . maybe ever."

"Your bed?"

"My bed." His light blue eyes rested hotly on her as he spoke, his voice slurred by passion. "And I discover a water nymph in it, sleeping on sheets of red silk." He lifted the long curls of her hair and wove his fingers through them. "I hoped you would come to trust me. I hoped you would come to my bed willingly, but I never dared hope you would come to me this soon, my Maggy, my beautiful Magdelena, not after the way your husband must have treated you."

He didn't know the half of it, and the more she thought about it, the more she was beginning to doubt that she did either. What had Wes done? A warning bell sounded in her brain. "Joshua . . ." She tickled a sensitive spot on the side of his ribs with one finger, caressing him almost absently as she talked. "You're quite sure this is your lodge?"

"You must have known." He frowned at her preoccupation with unimportant details when there were so many more interesting things to concentrate on.

"Does . . ." She faltered, not sure that she wanted to know. "Does the name Wesley James Dailey mean anything to you, and if so, what?"

"Magdelena, my darling, I am in no frame of mind for twenty questions." He sighed as he felt her stiffen resolutely in his arms. "But if it'll make you happy, then yes, the name Wes Dailey does mean something to me. We were friends in college. We kept in touch off and on over the years. He called me last year say, oh, I guess, about October, and told me he had purchased a lodge in Arizona and needed a partner to help bankroll renovations. I agreed and bought into the deal for a quarter share. After the lodge got back on its feet under new management, I was supposed to begin to realize a profit."

"And did you?" She knew the answer already.

"No." He played along. "As a matter of fact, I didn't. Wes called again and said there'd been more involved in the renovations and restorations than he'd originally thought. He said if I was interested in making a profit as soon as I'd expected, I'd have to buy in for another quarter share."

"Making your total a half ownership?"

"Yes," he said impatiently. "Magdelena, why all the questions about Whitewater Lodge?"

"Because Whitewater Lodge is the business my ex-husband Wes Dailey left to me, lock, stock, and barrel." His body tensed above her.

"*You* were married to Wes Dailey?"

"That's right." She certainly was awake now, and she certainly wished she weren't.

"You were *married* to Wes Dailey? I didn't even know he had a wife."

"He didn't either. Don't worry about it. Joshua, we need to talk about the lodge."

"You *were* married to Wes, as in no longer married?"

"Yes!" she shouted at him. Men could be so obtuse at times. "And if you repeat that same question one more time, I'm going to add you to the list of people I'd most like to strangle, right there after Wes, who, yes, I was married to and, thankfully, am no longer married to!"

"We can't both own the lodge," he said at last, rolling off her and pounding his hand against the bedpost in thought. "I have a signed contract from Wes stating very clearly just what I do and do not own, and furthermore just what I will own. I'll admit the lodge doesn't look like much now. When I made the trip out here to see what was being done with my money, I was ready to skin him alive too. But the place does have potential, and I thought, with the right management and with him out of the way—"

"But he isn't out of the way," she interrupted. "At least, he is, but I'm not, and I have papers in my possession saying that I own Whitewater Lodge. In fact, they're here in the lodge now. I gave them to my Aunt Deirdre to read—Oh, good heavens!"

"What is it?" he yelled, jerking reflexively. "Don't just scream like a banshee without giving more details. What is it?"

"Where's Bailey? Tell me your right-hand man doesn't live here with you at the lodge."

"But he does," he said, puzzled. "As of today. We only made two of the rooms habitable just today. He moves in tonight."

"Is he there now?" She closed her eyes in horror, praying that he wasn't. It would be poor payment for saving her life.

"He should be by now. I left him downstairs to fix himself a sandwich before bed. Magdelena, you're not worried about Bailey's reaction, are you?"

"I'm more worried about his life!" She catapulted off the bed, tossed on her robe, and dashed barefoot down the hall to the room she'd left Deirdre in. She could hear a cursing Joshua somewhere behind her, but she didn't wait for him. There wasn't time.

"Deirdre, wait!" she called as she started to open the door. "Don't do anything rash. It's Magdelena and friends."

A thud and a bloodcurdling scream rent the air just as she stepped into the room.

"Kiayyyyyeeeeeee!" Deirdre, clad in her pink flannel nightgown, was poised, taut and ready, her bare foot only inches from Bailey's face, exhibiting all the defensive skill she'd been able to master in three years of private karate lessons.

"What in hell is going on here?" Joshua gathered like a thundercloud beside Magdelena at the door.

"No, you don't. You're not going in there." She pressed her hand against the firm leanness of his stomach to stop him, her fingers unconsciously caressing the curling hair there. "Deirdre in a fighting frenzy is nothing to fool with."

Bailey slid out from under the ready-to-strike-again foot, his bare and slightly flabby midriff showing the mark from where that foot had been. He made for the door, looking like a comically wounded sumo wrestler in white boxer shorts and white cotton socks.

"I'm sleeping in the boathouse tonight, Josh," he called over his shoulder on his way downstairs. "But I'm warning you, I'm going to be hunting for another place to sleep and another place to work in the morning. You said you were were looking for some people to act as security for the grounds, but I didn't expect to find—and I don't like finding—some female Bruce Lee type camping out in my room."

Joshua watched Bailey disappear, then looked from Deirdre to Magdelena and back, his mouth gaping open. "I'd give the shirt off my back to know what just happened." He held up a hand. "I'll be back. Don't go anywhere." Racing down the stairs two at a time, he hurried to catch up with Bailey.

"Heel." Magdelena shook her aunt's shoulder as Deirdre followed Joshua. "Those were the two men I was telling you about."

"Good for them." Making sure Joshua was far enough away from the house, Deirdre closed and locked the door from the inside.

"Have you taken leave of your senses?" Magdelena demanded. "Those men saved my life. You can't lock them out!"

Something very solid hit the door on the run and rattled the knob ineffectually.

"I just did." Deirdre crossed her arms and proceeded to wait.

"Red?" A man's voice, devoid of its earlier humor, reached them from the other side. "This isn't funny. It's cold out here. Haven't you gotten your aunt muzzled or corralled or sedated or *something* yet?"

"Not quite," she called out loudly, whispering to her aunt in the next breath. "What are you doing? Why are you doing what you're doing?"

"Because I read the papers Wes left you concerning the lodge, and they don't say you own all of the lodge. They say you own all of the lodge that *he* owned, and in addition, you've assumed all of his debts. So your Mr. Joshua Wade could very well own a portion of the lodge."

"Well, locking him out isn't going to change anything."

"We can bide our time until I see his proof, until I can think of something."

"Magdelena!" Joshua pounded on the door. "Let me in or I swear I'm going to break down the door even if it means I'll have to pay for a new one."

"Let him in." Magdelena tried to move Deirdre aside. "Forget what I said about saving the lodge for me at all costs. Forget about the law being sacred and all that. I have a feeling he's more than just moderately angry."

"I wouldn't do that if I were you, Mr. Wade." Deirdre assumed her professional manner, speaking to him as if he were a jurist who needed further instruction. "That would be breaking and entering, and if you did that I would be forced to call the police. In fact, I'm only inches from calling the police now. You say that you own Whitewater Lodge, but so far we've seen no proof of your claims. In fact, we've seen claims to the contrary. My niece, Magdelena, has proof that she owns the lodge, and frankly, as it is her only means of making a living for herself, she's not about to let it go to a complete stranger just on his say-so. Therefore, until you can provide the authorities with proof—"

"Correction." He was standing very close to the door, enunciating carefully so that his meaning wouldn't be misunderstood. "You aren't inches away from calling the police, you're miles from it, at least five miles, because the phone bill was one of the things Wes didn't pay with the money I sent him to run my half of the lodge. However, if it'll make you feel any better, I'll go and call the police myself. They know me and they'll tell you that I'm the new owner of Whitewater Lodge."

"I'm afraid hearsay doesn't hold water in a court of law, Mr. Wade," Deirdre interjected knowledgeably. "Do you have any other proof?"

"Not on me!" He sounded like an injured buffalo. "I'm half naked. Where would I keep important papers if I did have them?"

Magdelena peered out from the front window at him. He was hopping up and down on first one foot and then the other to keep warm.

"Actually, I do have papers," he continued. "But they're in my lawyer's safe and in case you hadn't noticed, it's well after midnight on a Friday night. I won't be able to get them until Monday morning."

"That'll be fine." Deirdre withdrew from the door, apparently satisfied with the delay. "And in the meantime I'm sure you'll be comfortable in the boathouse with whatshisname. There are only two beds in the lodge fit to sleep in anyway and they're occupied."

"I noticed." He muttered the last words at the door frame.

"I'm letting them inside, Deirdre." Maggy reached for the doorknob.

"If you do, that will compromise our position here," Deirdre warned her. "Letting the alleged owner inside as if he had a right to be here would signify that we agreed to the validity of his allegations. You do that and I shall be forced to withdraw as your legal defense in the case."

Maggy grimaced and petted the solid wood door, sympathizing with Joshua, scantily clothed out in the cold night air. "You realize, of course, that that's blackmail?"

"And you realize that that means I'll have to sleep outside, by myself, in the boathouse?" Joshua put his two cents in, hoping to sway the tide in his favor.

"Would you rather fight Aunt Deirdre to sleep in one of the beds in here?" she asked him dejectedly.

"I'd rather fight with a mountain lion and sleep with a porcupine." He groaned in resignation. "Truthfully, I'd rather sleep with you."

"Coming, Magdelena?" Deirdre asked.

Tapping on the door in Morse code, which she just knew he wasn't going to be able to decipher, Magdelena turned away. "You have a hard heart, Deirdre." There was a point after which no appeal was possible . . . not through regular channels, anyway.

Four

Twenty long minutes later Magdelena dressed quickly and tiptoed downstairs to the front door, opening it with one hand and an elbow. She felt as if she were running away from home. Two thick wool blankets were tucked under her arms while a six-pack of beer and a bag of tortilla chips dangled from her hands. She'd also located half a bag of beer nuts and a container of avocado dip, and for want of more hands had tucked them precariously under her chin. All she had to do now was get out of the house and quietly make her way in the dark to the boathouse. Simple. Unless you considered that she was loaded down worse than Santa Claus on the night before Christmas, and that she'd never been known for either her grace or her night vision. She eased the door shut and carefully made her way out to the boathouse, seeing it from an entirely different perspective this time.

"Joshuaaaa," she sang out hopefully, and knocked on the boathouse door with her foot.

"Hark." A mocking voice came from within. "I hear

the call of a white-breasted, red-headed trouble bird. What do you think, Bailey? Shall we let it in and see what it wants?"

Bailey mumbled something Magdelena wasn't sure she wanted to hear, then said gruffly, "Tell it to fly south and take its attack vulture with it."

Magdelena kicked the door again, crying out and dropping the six pack when she stubbed her toe. "Joshua, let me in, please. Don't you want to see what I've liberated from your stores?"

"You're admitting they *are* my stores?" he said with surprise, opening the door a crack and sending a thin sliver of light into the darkness.

"I'm ready to concede that they might be, if only you'll let me in." She leaned against the door frame, balancing her load with the help of the wall. "Come on. Be a sport."

"Why should I?" He wasn't ready to forgive her yet. "Bribe me with something."

She tried not to think of the one bribe that, judging from past experience, he might be willing to accept. "How about an apology?" she offered as substitute. "She really should have let you back in."

"And you, with your two broken arms, couldn't possibly have opened the door yourself."

"Have a heart!" She was beginning to have a real empathy for his earlier predicament, her exposed fingers turning blue from the cold. "You heard her say she'd leave us alone in our legal mud puddle if I did that. Actually, Wes is our common enemy. She'll see that in the morning. Besides, I told you I'd be back soon. It isn't my fault you didn't wait until she went upstairs so I could unlock the door."

"In a pig's eye." He had come to stand very close to his side of the door, talking into the crack, obviously enjoying the role reversal.

"I did tell you," she insisted. "In Morse code so

Deirdre wouldn't catch on. What's the matter? Weren't you ever a Boy Scout?"

The door creaked open slowly, revealing Joshua a tantalizing little bit at a time.

"Do I look like a Boy Scout?" Leaning casually against the inner door frame, he crossed his arms over his chest, covered by a skin-tight white T-shirt, and awaited her reply.

Magdelena licked her lips, finding her throat had gone dry, her mind blank. Boy Scouts were, to her way of thinking, little boys with short clipped hair and innocent eyes, wearing freshly laundered khaki uniforms that always looked like one size was supposed to fit all, but rarely did. The person standing before her, whom no one by any stretch of the imagination could describe as a boy, was no Boy Scout.

His sandy blond hair fell in natural waves, down over arched gold eyebrows, almost into his eyes, eyes that were giving her the once-over in a very innocent fashion. The rest of him didn't resemble any Boy Scout she'd ever met either, even though his darkly tanned skin, which contrasted sharply with the white T-shirt, did look as though he spent a great deal of his time outside. Even if he had covered his bulging muscles with a uniform top and replaced the blue jeans that hugged his long legs with khaki pants, she thought there was something about him that would make anyone sure he didn't spend his spare time helping little old ladies cross the street.

"I suppose you don't." Her voice had lowered to a throaty purr all by itself, her eyelids half open, mesmerized by her own thoughts of him. She was dreaming again.

"Do you think I could join if I did my good deed for the day and let you in?" He stood back and motioned for her to enter, a self-satisfied smile curling the corners of his mouth.

"We do need to talk." She glanced at Bailey, who was immersed in a western novel, ignoring them both. "And I do mean talk."

"That's too bad." He grinned. "I had hoped to let you in so that we could do other things. But you're probably right. We do need to get a few things settled before anything else. Business before pleasure and all that. Besides, I don't think Bailey would take kindly to being thrown out of yet another house." He spied the beer cans she was trying to pick up off the ground while juggling the remainder of her booty. "Although—"

"Joshua!" She dropped the avocado dip from shaking fingers, letting it fall with a sickening green splat onto the concrete.

"Better put some newspapers under your trouble bird's cage," Bailey said, still seeming to read, his face deadpan and devoid of the humor she could see in Joshua's expression.

"Have a beer, Bailey." Joshua winked at the older man and tossed him a can. "In fact, have several beers. Drink up."

"I came to discuss business," Maggy repeated pointedly, wondering if the excuse sounded as lame to them as it suddenly did to her. Nobody discussed business after midnight. "But maybe I should just wait until morning." She piled the blankets and tortilla chips and nuts into Joshua's waiting arms. "It really is kind of late and you both probably want to get back to bed."

"*I'd* like that," Joshua said with a grin. "But Bailey here is having trouble sleeping on a strange sofa. It's difficult to relax on something not wide enough for your shoulders. Maybe another beer would help him to relax. Have another beer, Bailey." He set another beside the first and inched over toward Magdelena.

"Sorry about that." She really did feel guilty. "That's another reason I came out. I wanted to tell you that you could sleep in the lodge if you want to. Deirdre's pretty hard to sway when she's confronted directly, but she falls short when presented with a *fait accompli*. So if you decide to come back in, I'll just leave the door unlocked." She was backing out of the boathouse one slow step at a time, her eyes never leaving an advancing Joshua. "The front door, that is. My bedroom door wouldn't have a lock on it, would it? And even if it did, you'd most likely have the key, wouldn't you?" She was rambling, stumbling over her tongue and the cement doorstep in her confusion.

Joshua caught her before she fell backward, his hands securely holding her by her shoulders. "Did you forget your contact lenses inside the lodge, Maggy?"

She shook her head no. His face was in sharp and breathtakingly detailed focus. "Why?"

The tiny crinkling lines at the corners of his eyes became more pronounced as he chuckled. "Because you seem to be having trouble seeing where you're going."

And even more trouble seeing what she was doing. Why had she come? She mentally blocked the answer to that one and tried to pull away from his grasp. "It's not just my normal sight that's bad. It's my foresight too. The only kind of seeing that I seem to be any good at is hindsight, and right now I'm seeing very clearly that I should have trusted Deirdre's instincts and stayed inside."

"Funny thing about instincts." He ran one hand delicately up the line of her jaw to a spot near her ear, caressing her throat gently before skiing artfully down the erogenous zone of her neck like a contestant in a giant slalom. "They just do their thing without your having to stop and think about them." He stopped when he reached the rising and falling swell of her breasts, visible above her V-neck sweater. "I'm of the opinion that people ought to follow their instincts a little more often and analyze their feelings a little less often. What do you think?"

Think? She'd stopped thinking in order to devote all her attention to feeling. "I think I'm in way over my head, and I think I'll just head on back to the house, maybe make myself a cup of hot chocolate, try to get some sleep." She she would, *after* an icy shower. She tried to back away from his fingers, which were making intricate designs on her soft skin. His movements were only barely outside of Bailey's line of vision.

"You don't want to do that." The expression on his face was telling her clearly that he dared her to break contact and deny that she wanted to stay. "There's too much caffeine in chocolate, and besides, take my word for it, we don't have any in the house. What you need is a beer. Come on back in and I'll get you one. It's very good for insomnia, isn't it, Bailey?" He tossed the comment over his shoulder. "I can see Bailey's getting sleepy already. His book's ready to fall out of his hand. I'm sure *he'd* have no trouble sleeping if he tried. And I have other remedies for you to try if the beer doesn't work, Magdelena."

She just bet he did!

"And I have somewhere else to be." Bailey stood, Bailey being no fool, and tossed down the rest of his beer.

"Oh, no, you don't." She wasn't about to let the one thing standing between her and irresistible temptation walk out the door and leave them alone.

"Where's he going?" she asked Joshua as Bailey trudged out the door without so much as a "good luck" in her direction.

"I would imagine he's off to beard the lioness in her den. Your Aunt Deirdre wounded his pride along with his stomach. Bailey's not going to let that go." He closed the door behind Bailey and drew her into the room. "And I'm not going to let you go, not until you tell me why you're so frightened of the way you feel about me, why you trust me one minute and won't trust me the next. . . ." He touched the tip of her chin, then dropped his hand once the contact had been made. "Or trust me with your feelings, which I would never willingly hurt, which is why I let you in here tonight without exacting payment for being thrown out of my own home."

"You did exact payment," she corrected him. "You made me stand outside in the cold for a good five minutes before you let me inside."

"At least you have a shirt on, and warm pants. And I didn't exact the payment I wanted to demand from you, the remuneration that would have given me the most pleasure. Do you want to know why?"

"Tell me." Her Benedict Arnold of a mouth betrayed her better judgment, speaking before she had time to think what compensation he could request for being locked out of the house.

"Because as much as I want to finish the dream we started together upstairs, I'm afraid to. I'm afraid if I levy one night in your arms as payment of your debt, then one night is all I'd ever get. And I want a great deal more than one night. I realized that, Red, about five minutes after I first set eyes on you." He paused and looked down at her, his voice touched with not just a little awe. "I'm prepared to give you the time you need . . . and possibly a great deal more than that, to get more than just that one night, to get you to come to me willingly, to get you to stay in my life."

"I don't understand." It almost sounded as if he

was prepared to sacrifice something very dear to him. But what was it? And why would he sacrifice anything for her?

"Let me ask you something." He pressed his lips together, a frown settling over his face. "Was your aunt exaggerating when she said that you needed Whitewater Lodge to make a living for yourself?"

She didn't feel the need to lie to him. The embarrassment she'd felt earlier was gone. How had he accomplished that? "No, she was telling you the truth about that. It was how I planned to make a living for myself."

"Was?" he said pointedly.

"Was, because she wasn't telling you the truth about everything before. I don't own all of Whitewater Lodge as I first assumed. I own all that Wes owned, which may be half . . . or even less. He may have had more than one other partner, in which case I may own his debts, but own nothing with which to pay them." It sounded even worse when she said it out loud.

"No," Joshua said firmly. "I can guarantee that the only other partner Wes had was and is me." He looked at her oddly. "And since I own only half of the lodge, then it's safe to assume you own the other, and thus a way to make a living for yourself . . . if you'll stay."

"As your business partner?" She darted anxious glances from his wide, sensual mouth up to see whether his blue eyes held a passionate or a professional interest. Business and pleasure wasn't a combination that mixed well for her, a fact she had learned through bitter experience.

Pulling Bailey's chair up for himself, Joshua drew her down onto the couch and faced her, kneading her fingers with his hands. "Why do I get the feeling that I'm walking a verbal tightrope with you, and that if I say one wrong word you'll walk out of my life without so much as a backward glance?"

She looked down at his hands, which had suffered to keep her skin intact. How could she not trust him? "I don't want to leave the lodge, and I think I'd have a hard time walking away from you without a great many regrets." She trembled with a wave of longing as he inclined his head to rest it on her shoulder. He was listening to her every word, trying to hear what she meant behind the words, silent, but expectant, sensing that there was more to come.

"But?"

"But I don't want to get involved with a man who's also my business partner. I tried that before and it was a mistake, a big mistake." She turned her head to touch his, sharing her fears with him, this virtual stranger in terms of time—Joshua, who had never seemed like a stranger at all. "In the future I want to keep my personal life separate from my professional life. Because the last time I didn't, I had to leave everything behind when the relationship ended. My friends, my home, my career, my business contacts, my way to make a living. Everything that had been my life. I can't go through that again. I can't *risk* going through that again. If I let myself love again, and I lose the man . . ." She couldn't say Joshua's name, the possibility of having him too great a temptation to put into words, the chance of losing him once he'd been hers too distressing a possibility to think about. ". . . at least I won't lose everything else if all I own is mine alone."

He caressed her lowered head with his, his soft blond hair clinging to wild strands of red. "So what you're telling me is that if we're going to be permanent business partners, our relationship has to be strictly business. Is that it?"

That was it. She hadn't wanted to put it like that, but that was it. And it would be emotionally safer all around if they could come to that same agreement, if they could both agree to ignore rather than exploit the obvious chemistry brewing between them. She nodded.

"Does that mean if we *weren't* going to be business partners that you'd consider becoming my lover?"

The question was direct and unexpected. She jerked back from him in surprise, breaking the contact of their inclined heads and caressing hands. Talking about it wasn't going to make anything any easier.

"Well, theoretically speaking, possibly . . ." She was having some trouble speaking theoretically. "If and when I begin dating again, it would be best if I chose someone away from my business associates, don't you think?"

He didn't answer her as she expected, maintaining an amused silence even as he lifted her chin, forcing her to meet his direct gaze.

"I think the situation's gone far beyond that. I don't think you can choose another man because I think you've already made a choice. And I think you're evading the issue, Maggy m'darlin'. I'm not talking about some hypothetical situation with some as yet unknown suitor. To put it crudely, I'm asking if you'd sleep with *me* if we weren't business partners?"

Lying to him was out of the question. She wouldn't be convincing when her eyes surely held the truth that the rest of her body was confirming.

"*I* have no intention of selling my share of Whitewater Lodge to you or anyone else," she said firmly. "But if one of us was to, say, sell his share to the other or to someone else, then I suppose, maybe—"

"No supposing, Maggy. No maybes." He took her chin between his thumb and forefinger and moved her head from side to side. "I do not want to deal in anything but absolutes. I want to hear a definite yes or a definite no. If one of us was positively not going to own Whitewater Lodge, for whatever reason, would you or would you not go to bed with me, here, tonight, now?"

She squelched an impulsive urge to ask if she could call Deirdre in for a consultation. Something in Joshua's manner warned her that he wouldn't see the humor in it. Still . . . She tried to think about things objectively, trying not to think about the male hands that were rubbing up and down her arms and shoulders persuasively.

If Joshua didn't own the lodge, would really be willing to sell it to her, then yes, it would be possible to have a relationship with him. . . .

"It isn't that hard, Maggy," he prompted her. "Either you admit to wanting me, or you lie to us both and deny it. Either way, I'll do my best to go along with your wishes."

She bit her lower lip, wishing he weren't so temptingly near. Denying that she wanted him was going to sound ridiculous if she was actively engaged in admitting that she did want him.

"Yes!" The decision left her lips with a small explosion, its impact forcefully hitting them both. "If we didn't have a business relationship then yes, sorry though I'll probably be for saying so, yes, I *would* be tempted to make love with you. . . ." He was watching her intently, waiting. "Here. Tonight." She took a deep breath of air. It didn't feel like she was getting enough oxygen. "Now."

He released a long-held breath. "*That's* what I wanted to hear." He stood up, towering over her, making her eyes follow his every move as though her head were attached to him by a length of invisible string.

"Would you like to fill me in on what you're doing?" she asked, watching in fascination as he lifted the bottom of his T-shirt up, peeling it off his chest and over his head.

"This has nothing to do with my being locked out of my bedroom, Maggy," he said, his eyes searing hers with unsuppressed desire. "No more games tonight, m'love. I want us to share the kind of closeness that only a man and woman can know."

His voice became quieter, more determined. "Maggy, with the lodge in the state of disrepair it's in, and with the charter service lacking any summer bookings, we couldn't hope to sell to an outside party without major improvements. And you don't have enough cash to buy me out outright, not now. But if we both work to rebuild the lodge and its business, then I will guarantee that by the end of the summer we won't be running the lodge as co-owners. We will no longer be business partners. You have my word on it."

Maggy's expression was disbelieving. He wasn't going to sell his half of the lodge just to get a woman into bed, she'd never believe that. He wanted the lodge, she knew it. But she also knew, somehow, that what he promised, he meant. . . .

"Joshua, I can't believe you're serious," she said slowly, her eyes suddenly riveted to his hands, which rested on the waistband of his jeans.

"I've never been more serious about anything in my life, Maggy. I'll even sign a sworn statement to that effect in front of your Aunt Deirdre right now, if you'd care to go get her."

What could she say to that? Maggy wondered, a kind of desperation mixed with her own surprising need for this man. She murmured absently, "I'm not going to the lodge until I see whether Bailey comes out alive or not." Joshua grinned at her words, beginning to unroll two sleeping bags on the floor of the cabin.

"I'm glad, Maggy," he said with intensity, folding back the top sleeping bag after it had been arranged to his satisfaction. "Because I have more urgent things to do right now than try to explain to your aunt why I need legal papers drawn up at—" He leaned over to look at his watch lying on a nearby table—"2:30 in the morning." Half reclining on the sleeping bags, he pulled her to him with a sudden movement.

"How urgent?" she murmured, feeling a sensual languor wash over her as his sensitive fingers caressed the nape of her neck.

"Urgent enough to make me forget any sense of decorum I ever had. You don't want to make small talk either, do you, Maggy? What we have to say to each other with our lips will go unspoken tonight," he said with a passionate fervor that made Maggy's heart pound with excitement at the image his words produced in her mind.

"Ah, Maggy, Maggy mine," he whispered next to her ear, his warm breath brushing her tender skin with flame as he brought his lips down on hers and fulfilled the promise he'd made. With tiny, seductive kisses he outlined her rosy mouth, tasting her with delicacy, then deepening the embrace with the darting tip of his tongue. Maggy had never been the fainting type, but she felt herself swooning in Joshua's arms as she responded with her own rising passion to his demanding lips.

As her fingers began massaging his muscular back and shoulders, Joshua growled an inarticulate, pleading sound into her ear and ran wild, impatient hands up and down her back and around her waist. "I've got to see you, to touch you, Maggy," he muttered fiercely, and when he met with no resistance, tugged her sweater over her head and tossed it aside, his eyes locking with hers as he reached to touch her more intimately. Maggy breathed shallowly, lost in the dream of it, as his appreciative look made her shiver. His arms reached around her as he drew closer, unclasping the hooks of her bra and drawing the sheer beige lingerie away from her gently. The straps fell down over her shoulders, with the cups held in place only by her arms, which she'd dropped to her sides.

He smiled at her uncertainly, hopefully, and drew a big question mark with his forefinger over each breast, his finger slightly unsteady as it came into contact with her flesh.

She took a shaky breath and removed one strap, sliding it down over her elbow and forearm, slipping it off her wrist, all without exposing either breast.

"Making love was a casual pastime for Wes," she said softly," like eating breakfast or getting his shoes shined. Sometimes it seemed like he was only half there, as though his thoughts were elsewhere. But for me making love is very different. Sharing my body with a man, and all that means, is not something I do lightly or casually. I hardly know you, Joshua, and yet somehow this feels right." She slipped the other strap down, holding the bra on with hands cupped under her breasts. "I don't know how you feel, but—"

"You don't need to ask. I'll tell you." Taking his cue, he removed her bra almost reverently. "I'll show you." He brought her close, his mouth seeking hers in a kiss that imparted not only passion but a recognition of the reservations she'd overcome to let him be there. "I think I'm falling in love with you, and I'm not taking you, or your very beautiful body, lightly or casually. When I make love to you, neither one of us will be thinking of anyone or anything else. I guarantee it."

His mouth was warm and moist as he traveled from her lips to her breasts in slow stages, making stopovers at the soft-skinned tender spots behind both ears, at the pulse point that beat quickly at the side of her neck, and at the hollow at its base. Pushing her back to lie open to him on his make-shift bed, he lay next to her, sculpting her full breasts with knowing hands.

Her nipples rose of their own accord into his wait-ing palms, tingling as he curled his fingers around them. Replacing his hands with eager lips, he drew each ripe rose-red bud into his mouth, running his teeth across them with infinite care, using just enough pressure to create a slightly grating sensa-tion that was far more arousing than any softer touch would have been.

"Oh, Joshua . . ." Her mouth formed an O of plea-sure and she arched her back. With his impassioned caresses he was igniting womanly needs and feel-ings she'd never known, never even imagined. "Don't stop, please."

"I've just started," he promised in a voice throaty and low, his breath hot on her love-warmed skin. The shower of words and kisses continued as he lowered himself down on her body, taking unashamed delight in each new discovery of what pleased her, aroused her.

He pressed his lips to the delicate skin above her navel, then pulled away with a groan of soft regret. "We've got a small problem, Maggy m'love," he said quietly.

"What is it?" she whispered, reaching for him again, needing to feel his skin against hers, to revel in the caress of his furred chest against her sensi-tive fullness.

"Oh, Maggy mine," he murmured, burying his face in a handful of her long red hair, breathing deeply of its natural perfume. "I'm a complete and utter idiot for not thinking of this until now." His palms brushed tenderly over the pale smoothness of her stomach.

"What is it?" she asked again. Whatever it was, she knew she'd stopped hoping it would prevent them from making love to each other.

"Our problem, dear Maggy, is that you're unprotected. Nothing but that would keep me from making you mine tonight. But as much as I want you—and feel you want me—you're too precious to me to risk—"

Maggy touched his lips with her fingertips. "Oh, Joshua, you make me feel so—so cared for. And I do want you, in a way I never imagined wanting any man. I just want to sleep tonight in your arms, and dream my dream again. I know you'll make it come true very, very soon."

Before she could go on, Joshua pulled her into his arms and down onto the sleeping bags, embracing her as if he would never let her go. Their arms entwined, they held each other lovingly all night long.

Five

"The sun's coming up." Magdelena lay within the circle of his arms much later, watching the sun rise through an open window on the east side of the room. "Joshua?" The sound of his quiet, even breathing convinced her of what she'd suspected for the past ten or fifteen minutes. He was finally asleep.

Their closeness through the night had been wonderful and dangerously intoxicating. Lying spoon fashion on the quilted down bags, their bodies pressed together as if welded by need, they'd spent the night talking, laughing, and embracing, quietly sharing souls and secrets until a contented weariness slowed even that to an occasional whispered remark.

Disengaging herself from his arms and unwinding her hair from them both, Magdelena re-covered Joshua with the top sleeping bag and went in search of her clothes. She picked them up with a bemused expression. It had all happened so fast, the meeting and the courting, such as it had been, their near-lovemaking—a whirlwind of wild romance compressed into the space of a day. Had it been worth it, had she been right to respond to this man with such intimacy . . . such passion? She glanced at the sleeping man, curled up like a giant blond teddy bear around where her body had been.

It had been worth it, she decided, every scrape, every moment of uncertainty and fear. Loving him, letting him get close, had meant taking a risk, but with every word and deed he'd succeeded in convincing her that it was worth the gamble. She felt the rightness of it in her bones, even though she still knew very little about him. She'd learned that he was thirty-four, had a degree in business administration, and had taken a leave of absence from a prestigious executive position in Colorado, where he'd been raised and where his parents and four brothers and sisters still made their home. He'd wanted to branch out on his own, to work for himself for a change, to try his hand at something new.

What she didn't know was what his plans were going to be six months from now after their partnership was severed and, more important, how she would feel when it was time for him to go. Was it really necessary that he leave? She reached down to touch his fair hair, his face very, very young in repose. At that moment she felt she'd never want to part from him.

She left, postponing the war between her heart's desire and her mind's logic. There were other things she had to force herself to think about this morning. She quietly closed the door behind her and almost skipped back to the lodge. The sound of arguing voices, one high and determined, the other low and stubbornly obstinate, greeted her at the door.

"I say we use the money to buy playground equipment, picnic benches, an above-ground pool, and a few cribs and high chairs. And, if we're going to cater to families, we'll need to have good babysitters on staff."

Magdelena recognized Deirdre's high-handed, authoritative voice at once.

"And I say we use the money to buy a couple of regulation card and pool tables, a solid oak bar with some sturdy stools, eight or ten rifles for target practice to rent out to the *men* who'll be coming here, and maybe a couple of good bows for the archery range. And as long as we're talking about hiring anybody, we'd better make it a bartender."

"Oh, that's good," Deirdre's sarcastic drawl came again. "We're going to advertise Whitewater Lodge as a place for families to come, and you plan to offer them booze, weapons, and gambling."

"And I suppose you want to give a man who's just run a class three section of water a ride on a merry-go-round and put him to sleep in a crib with a babysitter hovering over to tuck him in!"

Magdelena pushed the door open and found the two contenders sitting across from each other at a dusty table which they'd dragged into the main hall. Both were still in last night's crumpled clothes, looking quite a bit the worse for wear.

Bailey puffed foul-smelling smoke from a cigar held tightly in one side of his mouth, his side of the table cluttered with a round container of chewing tobacco, a stubby pencil and pad of paper, and a bowl of taco chips.

Deirdre, on the other hand, a felt-tip pen clutched between her teeth, had covered her side of the table with wads of crunched-up paper, a telephone book, a coffee mug, and a bag of sunflower seeds, the sides of which had split in several strategic places, littering the table with seeds.

Leaning forward aggressively, their elbows on the

table, they looked like two top arm-wrestling champions settling down for the final bout.

"Before you two come out of your corners for whatever round you're in now, do you mind telling me something?"

The referee. The umpire. The deciding vote. They pounced on her, drawing her into the room, and proceeded to fire a barrage of questions at her from both sides with lightning speed.

"What do you think about advertising in all the local papers in Flagstaff, Prescott, and Tucson in this state, and then—"

"—setting up some campsites with running water and electrical hookups for the guys who want to rough it."

"And a chef. We really need a good chef. Maybe French. All that exercise out on the water will give people hearty appetites for—"

"—Hopi food. You ain't lived until you've tasted some traditional Hopi food like some of the local people cook around here. Rabbit corn bread, baked pumpkin, yucca pie if we can get a steady supply, and piñon nuts."

"Nuts!" Magdelena circled the table with the two combatants watching her. "You're *both* nuts. What did you do last night, knock each other senseless? The way my finances are, I'll be lucky if I can buy advertising in a high-school newspaper, and as far as all the other expenditures go, well, I have a few plans of my own for any money I may bring in. I plan to buy—" She cut herself off, realizing that Bailey was hanging on her every word. Joshua had hired him. Joshua had the right to tell him about the change in ownership before she made him any kind of a proposition herself. "I plan to buy some cleaning supplies first. We can't advertise for business until we're fit to open for business. And speaking of cleaning . . ." She darted suggestive glances at both Deirdre and Bailey. "Since you two seem to be on speaking terms, would you consider being on working terms and helping me out for the next few days?"

Bailey opened his mouth to respond, Magdelena assumed negatively, but was cut off as Deirdre answered for them both. "We've been working all night and we've got plans to continue today. Did you know that Bailey used to manage this place for the former owners long before Wes took over? That's how Joshua and he met. Bailey was out looking over his old stomping grounds when Joshua first came to see the property."

"I was fishing," Bailey added, "and I heard this cursing and bellowing and—"

"Anyway," Deirdre interrupted, "it appears your Mr. Wade didn't realize what Wes had gotten him into any more than you did. He was just lucky he checked into things before Wesley had a chance to make them worse. It does appear that you have a new partner, my dear." She offered this tidbit of information as if it were unimportant and yesterday's news. "So Bailey does have a few very good ideas on running the lodge. You'd do well to keep him on." She threw Bailey a grudging glance. "Though I still contend that if his ideas had been all that sound, the owners wouldn't have been forced to sell."

"I didn't hold the purse strings *then* either," Bailey defended himself, pointing his cigar at Deirdre. "And just because you do, lady, don't think that gives you the last word on everything, because you still have Joshua to clear it with." He shoved the cigar back between his teeth and puffed it at her. "And *he's* not going to go for baby cribs and French chefs."

Magdelena tapped Deirdre on the shoulder. "What purse strings?"

"If he's smart he won't go for rifles and bar stools either!" Deirdre shouted at Bailey.

"What purse strings?" Magdelena wedged her face in between the two of them.

"And what makes *you* an authority on running a lodge, woman?" Cigar smoke enveloped Magdelena's head.

"What purse strings?" she screamed over the smoke and din. "Did someone die and leave me a much-needed inheritance?"

"I have this little nest egg. Not much really," Deirdre said with a shrug. "Consider it a loan, if you like, or a one-time cash advance to cover the cost of my room and board any time I come to visit."

"I appreciate it, Deirdre, I really do." Magdelena hugged her aunt impulsively. "But if it's *my* loan, don't you think I ought to have some say in how it's spent?"

"Well, of course." Deirdre seemed surprised that her niece would even have to ask. "You and Joshua are the owners. Bailey and I are just the consultant and financial backers. Which reminds me, I need to go into town to check on some advertising, see if I can get a good deal for your dollar." She ran her fingers over the table, giving it a silent—and failing—grade on the white-glove test. "Meantime, you and Joshua should sit down and discuss who you're going to get to clean this place up."

"I've got some running around to do too," Bailey said. "If we want to reopen the rafting business this summer, we'll need to hire guides and pilots now. I know where a few of the old ones hang out, so I think I'll check in with Josh and see you ladies later."

Magdelena shifted her weight uncomfortably from foot to foot. "Deirdre, I need to speak to you before you go."

"No problem." She motioned Bailey back. "Give me a minute here and I'll take you into town with me. We haven't finished this conversation." She waited until he'd grunted a positive acceptance and slammed the door on his way out.

"What's up, Maggy dear? You look like you're walking on eggs."

"Joshua's agreed to sell his half of the lodge to me, if I can swing it, to someone else if I can't, by the end of the summer," she said without preamble.

"Magdelena . . ." Deirdre shrugged apologetically. "I do have a nest egg to invest, and I'll do what I can to help you. You know that. But, dear, it's more the size of a robin's egg than an eagle's, if you get my drift." Her eyes narrowed shrewdly. "And now that I think about it, how did you manage to get him to agree to a thing like that? If it's run properly, this place could net someone a tidy sum to live on, and if I recall correctly, your Mr. Wade wasn't too happy about being thrown out of his potential gold mine for even one night, let alone on a permanent basis."

Magdelena hadn't figured that one out herself, and yet he *had* said they wouldn't be partners by the end of the summer, and she had informed him that she didn't want to sell. "I can't explain it. All I know is that he said that's the way it would be if that's the way I wanted it."

"And that's the way you want it?" She wrinkled her nose at her niece. "Magdelena, I didn't get to be an attorney with the kind of reputation I've got by being unperceptive and obtuse."

Lovely memories of the previous night slid across Magdelena's mind's eye for a moment, bringing an undisguised look of longing to her face until she dismissed the daydream. "It'll be better this way, safer, no complications," she promised them both. "You'll have to admit that my past experience with business partners leaves something to be desired, which is why I can't understand for the life of me why you're pushing this one so hard." She switched tactics, putting Deirdre on the defensive. "You were the one who locked him out of the lodge last night. Now you're after him as a permanent resident and you haven't even seen the legal papers entitling him to be here. Whatever happened to sacred law and all that?"

"Put on temporary hold until Monday when his lawyer is in the office," Deirdre said calmly. "Though I don't think I'm going to be in for any major surprises. Which is why I think that while Bailey and I are in town it might behoove you to sit down with your temporary partner and discuss how you'd like to spend your small grant."

"Loan."

"Manna from heaven."

She gave in. "All right. When do you think you'll be back?"

"Probably not until all the upstairs bedrooms have been cleaned or until you run out of supplies, whichever comes first. There are some in the kitchen, and I'll bring you back some more. See you early this evening."

Magdelena gave up three hours and thirty minutes after Deirdre's sports car had pulled out of the drive with Bailey in the passenger's seat, both occupants still arguing at the top of their lungs.

She'd planned on working until Joshua came to find her, ostensibly to talk about present expenditures and future plans. But after all this time—four bedrooms cleaned out of a possible filthy ten and six fingernails broken, she tossed in the towel, literally, deciding it might be in the best interests of her dishpan hands to take the bull by the horns and search him out. He couldn't still be in bed, could he? She mentally reviewed their earlier conversations to determine if he'd said anything to give her a clue to his whereabouts today. The image of him lying still abed, and of the promises they'd made for later there, brought a gleam to her eyes and a private smile to her lips.

"Before you put all the soap and water away to attend the ball, Cinderella, do you think you might come out of your reverie long enough to tackle one final cleaning project?"

Magdelena's head snapped up, aware only that the Joshua standing before her was not just a part of an elaborate daydream.

Dressed in light blue shorts and running shoes, he looked better even than she remembered, his fair-haired legs covered in wood shavings and sweat, his bare chest bathed in a fine film of perspiration, the dust and debris he'd obviously been working in clinging to him like a second skin.

"When you didn't come in this morning, I thought you might still be sleeping." She pushed the bucket of soapsuds aside with her foot, wishing she could remember what the question was. The comfortable familiarity she'd felt with him last night fled as she was confronted again by the power of his masculinity.

"Bailey had other ideas in mind," he said. "Like repairing the rafts and the dock. I've been outside working all morning." His eyes bored holes through her, making her wish she'd covered up the emerald green leotard she wore for working out with more than a fashionably old and torn sweatshirt.

Her legs were bare, the sides of the leotard cut high to reveal skin all the way up to her hipbones. And it didn't seem to matter to him that, for the moment, all of her was covered in several layers of dust and grime and sweat, or that her long red hair was twisted into an uncomplimentary knot atop her head.

Instead, he looked at her as he had last evening, in that intensely personal way of his that made her feel as though she was the most desirable and beautiful woman on earth.

"You must realize that I've been waiting for you to come out and find me." His voice was gentle and inquiring, his hands mimicking it as he reached out to caress a patch of bare shoulder peeking through a tear in her sweatshirt. "Why didn't you come?"

"I was waiting in here for you," she admitted. "I thought I'd clean until you came to find me." She picked up the cleaning rag and twisted it between nervous fingers, giving her hands something to do besides reach out to him. "I've been hoping you'd arrive for at least four bedrooms."

The tension was broken, his smile at the unintended reminder of the previous night's postponed intimacy full of sensual promise. "I don't know if we have the time to sample *four* bedrooms before our keepers come back. Even I have my limitations. But I'm willing to give it a try if you are," he said and winked.

She frowned in mock outrage, and then both of them laughed.

"Are you finished here?"

She lifted a bottle of light vegetable oil and a clean rag from the carryall holding her cleaning supplies. "I'll be finished with all I planned to do today as soon as I oil the furniture in this room. What about you? Didn't you say you needed something cleaned?"

"The only thing I was hoping you'd offer to bathe was me." He chuckled. "But that will keep. I tell you what. Why don't I help you oil the furniture first and then you can help me scrub my back next? If you're as thorough with a bath brush as you are with a scrub brush, neither one of us will have the energy or the inclination to go back to work in here later."

She fought down what remained of her shyness. "You're on." She poured oil onto the cloth and handed it to him. She positioned him in front of a thirsty-looking dresser, then went to work on the bedposts.

"We could work on the same piece together," he suggested, whipping the rag over wood with lightning speed.

"Not on your life." She grinned at him slyly. "I want to finish the work. If I don't, you don't get your back scrubbed." Or anything else, she thought.

"Then you're not going about it the right way." He finished the dresser and joined her on the same side of the bed. "No need to be stingy with the oil. If we run out, I'll buy more . . . tomorrow. Here, let me help you." He took the bottle of oil from her and poured a liberal amount onto her cloth, dribbling it onto her hands and wrists at the same time. "You pour lots of it on, like this . . ." He wiped the cloth across the headboard quickly. "This wood needs an oil bath, it's so dry. Then just wipe off the excess. There." He finished with the headboard and looked up at her expectantly.

"What do I do with all the extra?" She lifted her arms and pushed up the sleeves of her sweatshirt as oil trickled down her forearms.

"Give it to a friend." He wiped a finger down her arm. "Or keep it yourself. Why worry about a little extra? You can use it for other things." He poured a generous palmful of oil into his hands and rubbed them together. "For example, it's great stuff if you want a suntan. Of course you have to put it on skin, and you have to uncover the skin that you put it on." He pulled the sweatshirt over her head and tossed it into the carryall. "And it's perfect for dry hair. Women pay copious amounts of money for hot oil treatments for their hair." He undid the clasp that held her hair in place and let the hair cascade down. He then rubbed the oil into her shoulders, which were left bare by the leotard's thin straps. "And I hear tell that it's miraculous for dry skin. Do you have any dry skin, Red?" He slid his hands down her arms. "Not there? How about here?" He massaged the skin at her elbows with strong, circular strokes. "My mother used to put baby oil on her elbows. And while this isn't exactly baby oil, it's not bad, and it's entirely natural. The label says so. Very good for your elbows, I'll bet. Mother used to use it on her knees too." He proceeded to demonstrate, working his way up from her kneecaps, massaging her thighs from hipbone to knee, traveling ever inward until his hands brushed her inner thighs.

"You're not going to tell me your mother used baby oil there," she said, her breath quickening.

"I wouldn't know." He grinned. "You'd have to check with my father on that one. But I wouldn't be surprised. I do have four brothers and sisters, you know, and in case you hadn't guessed by now, they don't spring full-grown from a cabbage patch."

"I believe we had this discussion last night." Her lips twitched.

"I believe we did. It's also rumored that this oil can be used for very sensual massage." He slipped his fingers under the straps of her leotard and tugged them down over her oiled shoulders. "Want to try it out?"

Maggie colored slightly at the idea but her shining eyes gave Joshua his answer.

"Do you mean test it scientifically, like in quality control?" she murmured.

"With an emphasis on quality," he promised. "Do

you have any wood floors that need oiling so that we can do two things at once, and thereby truthfully tell our truant officers that we worked all day? Or shall we just look for a bed that needs changing anyway, and then lie about our activities when they get back?"

She curled oil-slick fingers around his bare arm. "We could use your bed, and then just say we were engaged all afternoon in upper-management relations."

Joshua stopped to retrieve the bottle of oil and hurried her to his room. "Onward to the upper management conference room."

The room was just as they'd left it the night before, the blankets turned back temptingly, the mattress soft and inviting.

"You'll excuse me for a moment, ma'am, if I remove my tie? These conference rooms are always so hot." He whipped off the light blue shorts, kicked off his shoes, and stood at the side of the bed, beautifully, powerfully naked, enjoying the fascinated appraisal she couldn't help but give him.

"And so stuffy too." She began to undo the decorative elastic belt at her waist.

"Allow me." Standing very close beside her, he stripped the leotard from her slim figure and dropped it onto a chair. "After all, we need an uncluttered surface to work on if I'm to evaluate the product *adequately.*" After they sank onto the bed, he lifted the bottle of oil several feet above her and tilted it so that a liberal amount flowed out and splashed down onto her.

"Let me rub it in," she suggested a bit breathlessly, "and see if it breaks down under heat . . . and friction."

He watched, unmoving, his own breathing growing labored and heavy as she smoothed the oil over her breasts, spreading it in wide circles until her skin gleamed, the oil glistening as she moved, her nipples growing taut.

"I think you missed a spot." She lifted her hips ever so slightly, arching them toward the bottle held loosely in his hand. "Joshua?"

He licked his lips and poured more of the oil onto her stomach. She stroked the slippery liquid down over her abdomen, moving her hands sensuously down either side of her hips.

"I may need some collaboration on this from Quality Assurance," she purred, gliding her fingers up and down her oily thighs. She rolled over when he joined her so that she could anoint him with every touch. "Do you have someone in mind I could call in to test the product?"

"Do I!" He embraced her passionately, rubbing his body back and forth against hers until the bodies of both shimmered in the light. "I know just the man." He groaned as she began caressing him, her fingers slippery smooth as they skimmed the surface of his skin. "I *am* just the man. Name of heaven, Magdelena, you ought to patent those fingers. They're unique."

She tilted her head back as he mouthed the words into her neck, sucking small round circles of her skin into his mouth until she was marked as his.

"My personal stamp of approval," he said. "You've been graded A-One."

Maggie moaned with the unfamiliar, outrageous pleasure of it all, then whispered, "I don't think you've tested it *quite* thoroughly enough." She wriggled under him as he positioned his strong body directly over hers, no longer trying to hold his weight off her. She could feel the heat inside her growing, the need to have him within her increasing.

"Patience, sweet, sweet Magdelena, my very well-oiled angel. We'll test it as often and as long as you like. Soon. But we have to go slowly, slowly. . . . We have to make sure it's done right." He moved his hand over the upthrust point of one breast, across the slim waist, around the contour of her hip and to the triangle of red-gold hair, his fingers caressing her, stroking the throbbing center of her desire, his touch sending pulsations of tingling white-hot urgency through her body.

"Very, very slowly," he repeated, as she sought to increase the tempo of his movements. She writhed under his ministrations, her head thrown back, her lips parted in a passion that was just under the surface, ready to erupt.

"Not just yet. Not yet, my Magdelena of the talented fingers." He held both of her hands in his free one as she reached to touch him, as she sought to bring him to the same hungry, yearning state that gripped her. He brought her hands up to his lips with fervent kisses and half-audible promises, his other hand teasing her to a frenzied level of desire that could be contained no longer.

The sweet agony shattered her like crystal hit with precisely the right musical note, leaving her body trembling, out of control, until he brought her back to a plane of consciousness just a little short of heaven.

He cradled her to him, his long legs pressed along the backs of hers, his arousal evident against her back, his arms wrapped securely around her shoulders. He rocked her gently back and forth until her breathing slowed to somewhere near normal.

"What do you say we take that shower now," he murmured, "and then repeat our Quality Assurance tests again, to the limit this time?"

She moved her lips in an attempt to speak coherently. "Before or after Bailey and Deirdre get back and discover we've been whiling away the afternoon using up all the hot water?"

He laughed softly, then led her from his bed and into the shower. As she advanced on him, scrub brush in hand, he reached out and slapped her teasingly on the fanny.

"It's about time we let our 'financial planner' and our 'consultant' know who's really in charge here. Rank has its privileges, one of which is rights to all the shower time we want without kicks, comments, or complaints," he said firmly.

Six

"You rat! Aahhhhhhgghhh!" Magdelena dropped the bath brush and drew her arms around her as Joshua turned off the pleasantly warm water and blasted her, after she'd maneuvered him into a corner of the shower, with a stinging spray of icy cold. "Turn it off!" she begged. "Turn it off, please, or you're going to ruin our afternoon!"

He chuckled and moved to stand between her and the frigid blast of cold water. "On the contrary." He lifted his long arms to touch the shower ceiling, letting the water run down his arms, across his chest, down his sides and over his groin. "If I don't take a cold shower now, before I take you back to bed, we'll have a very short and definitely ruined afternoon."

"You could always jump into the Colorado." She huddled in a semi-protected corner of the shower.

"Not unless I take you with me for company."

"I hate cold water," she informed him, reaching around him to try to nudge the hot water tap. "So much so that I'm going to leave unless you do something about it posthaste."

The warm torrent was immediately back again, and his cold body all that remained of the freezing shower.

"I could get you warm." She began snuggling closer to him, letting the water cascade over her hair. "You'd enjoy it. Honest."

"Is that a promise?" He leaned closer to her inviting warmth, his previous thoughts of delaying the inevitable erased.

"Do you need it in writing?"

He wedged her nude body between his and the shower wall, pressing her against the white ceramic tiles. "I don't think so." He pretended to consider it. "I don't think either your Aunt Deirdre or her legal briefs would fit in here with us, not unless she decided to do a little impromptu remodeling and kick a hole in the wall." He flashed her a devilish grin. "Which would create something of a draft."

"Not to mention something of a view."

He moved her away from the wall and cupped her buttocks in possessive hands. "We'd best not invite her in with us then. I have no intention of making your showers a popular spectator sport for our lodge guests. I fully intend to keep the sight of your beautiful body all to myself."

"*Only* the sight?" she stood on tiptoe, her face close to his as she raised her eyebrows with dramatized suggestiveness. "I wouldn't have thought you to be much of a fan of spectator sports. You seem to be more of a participant type." She gave him a sisterly, passionless peck on the cheek and backed away to the opposite wall. "However, if *seeing* is all you're interested in, now that I've satisfied your voyeuristic fantasies, maybe I'd better get out."

Her avenue of escape was instantly blocked by one powerful arm, her refuge in the corner of the shower crowded as he pursued and held her there with the bulk of his dripping wet body. He held himself just a little aloof from her, his chest and thighs and hips only millimeters from touching hers, forcing her to anticipate just when he would choose to close that very small distance, heightening her awareness of the sexual tension that sparked back and forth between them.

"You haven't begun to satisfy my many and varied fantasies, Red." He ended the waiting, reaching around her to retrieve the soap from its dish on the shower wall, the hair on his arm brushing against her shoulder in the barest hint of contact. "Most of which require dry land and a clean body to perform well."

He held his arms widely outstretched, leaving himself open and vulnerable to her, giving her the freedom to touch him where she would and when she chose. "I'm putty in your hands, Red. Dirty putty. Covered-with-sweat-and-wood-shavings putty. Overly oiled putty. Anxious-and-eager-to-get-back-to-bed putty."

"I get the picture." She took the soap from his hand and rubbed it to a lather in her palms, applying it to his six-foot-three-inch frame with seductive slowness, an inch at a time.

He stood very still, sharing the delight she was taking in his body, watching her intent expression as she smoothed the creamy soft lather down his collarbone and over each broad shoulder. Working up another handful of soap, in much the same way as an artist mixes paints for each area of a canvas, she slathered the cleansing froth under his arms and across his chest to his back until he looked as though he were decorated with mounds of whipped cream.

"Magdelena . . ." he purred. "I'm starting to itch."

"I'll . . . scratch it in a minute. I'm not finished."

She lightly scored his body with her fingernails and rubbed him with the tips of her fingers, scrubbing and scouring him with a fascinated interest.

"You're looking awfully pleased with yourself about something," he observed. "You're not planning to take pictures and use me in a soap commercial, are you?" His hands clenched together convulsively as she circled his flat nipples with soapy fingers and danced a bubbly staccato down the graceful hills and valleys of his ribcage to the flare of his heretofore unsoaped pelvis.

"I don't think you're wholesome enough for that."

His eyes narrowed with pleasure as she scooped up two handfuls of suds from his chest and stood slightly back, deliberating about how best to approach the unwashed part of him. "If I'm not wholesome, Red, then just what am I?"

"One thing's for certain." She cloaked him in a fig leaf of lather. "You're the largest bath toy *I've* ever had the opportunity to play with."

His breathing quickened as she began rubbing the fig-leaf motif away.

"You'd better seize the opportunity then," he ordered. "Because if you make me stay in this water much longer, I'm going to shrivel up like a prune . . . all over." He stood, his legs quaking ever so slightly as she dropped to her knees on the shower floor and proceeded to stroke soft lather onto the springy blond hair at his groin, hiding his rigid masculinity once more in a frothing mountain of sweet-smelling soapsuds.

"I can't see that there's any danger of that happening. This bath toy seems to thrive on water." She dabbed at a few of the bubbles.

"Magdelena . . . it's *not* the water." He sucked in a series of uneven breaths as her fingers slid down the length of him and around to the softer, rounder parts of his male anatomy. "Maggy, I'm clean enough to pass any kind of an inspection you'd care to give me."

"Your thoughts aren't." She smiled mischievously up at him, still massaging him with slippery, knowing fingers.

"Take my word for it," he advised in a voice rasping with barely leashed desire. "Further washing in that vicinity will only make the condition of my dirty mind worse. Maggy, aren't you through yet?" He groaned and pulled her against his well-lathered body.

"I will be as soon as I'm as clean as you are. Here . . ." She moved back and forth in the tight hold of his embrace until they were both covered with lather, her breasts dripping with the milky froth, her thighs and belly squishing noisily, seductively as they made contact with his. ". . . this should save time."

"Woman, I swear, you're as slick as an army of snails and about as speedy!"

"Snails?" She dug her fingernails playfully into the upper swell of his buttocks. "Snails! I don't usually succumb to the turn of a pretty phrase, but that doesn't mean you couldn't try. Snails!" She closed her eyes and sputtered as he lifted her into the shower's direct spray and held her against him until the water had rinsed them both clean.

"I'll try," he promised. "Later. After my full concentration has returned to my brain. Just now I think I've lost all but the rudiments of speech." He pulled her from the shower and towel-dried her vigorously, bringing a rosy blush to her skin. "Come on, Red." He wound the towel turban style around her hair. "Take your bath toy to bed."

"I thought you'd never ask." Jumping into the middle of his mattress, she rolled over onto her stomach and managed a stifled scream as he landed on top of her and pulled her over on top of him.

"Thought I'd never ask!?" He tickled the sides of

her ribs with fast-moving fingers, bringing her to a laughing, giggling fever pitch, a torment that didn't stop as his fingers moved from her sides to continue the sweet, hot torture elsewhere. "I've been asking, pleading, *begging* for you for hours."

"Poor neglected baby. I'm here now."

"So you are. And right where I want you." Dropping his head to hers, he moved his lips over her mouth, stilling the residual laughter and the throaty moan that came when he reached for the veil of golden-red curls at the center of her femininity, rubbing and stroking her with the heel of his hand, tormenting her as she had him.

"And you want me to beg right along with you, right?" She arched herself against his fingers, seeking more of the delicious sensation.

"No need to beg." He lowered his lips to her breasts, teasing the already erect nipples to even sharper points of desire. "A single hint that you might be as crazy for me as I am for you would be sufficient."

"Is this hint enough?" She threaded her fingers slowly through the blond shag of his hair and brought his head up to within reach of her mouth. Tasting him with parted lips and an insistent tongue, she searched for and quickly found a response to match the one growing to out-of-control proportions within her.

He swiftly took care of protecting her, and when she was moving over him with an erotic choreography known to her only on an instinctive level, she guided him into her, making him a part of her as she had never made anyone else a part of her, joining him in flesh, in shared laughter, in need . . . in a belief that she could trust him with much more than joint worship of bodies.

"You realize, don't you, how crazy this is?" she whispered the tiny doubt that suddenly assaulted her, hoping for some emotional reassurance to go along with the physical. "I came to Arizona to find a new life in my work. Instead, all I want to think about is how you touch me, make me burn for your touch."

He crushed her to the strength of his chest and rolled over so that she lay under his body, his fierceness pushing her deep into the soft bedding. His eyes glittered and his voice was thick with a passion ready to explode. "I feel the same thing. I'm a part of you now, and you're in my blood, under my skin. That's the way I want it to stay. Always. No matter what happens in the future. Remember that, Maggy mine. Remember that I love you."

Trembling with a need to give as much as she was getting, she arched her back to meet his powerful thrusts halfway, her head thrown back in a passionate abandon that dislodged the towel, releasing her lustrous hair to fall free, cascading down onto the pillow. Responding to his body's every clue, she wrapped herself around him, moving fluidly with him and apart, holding him within her, loving him until their mutual ecstasy exploded, blotting everything else out but the sound of her name as he called it and moaned it and whispered it, and finally, at last, breathed it almost inaudibly into her ear.

"Magdelena . . . Magdelena . . . Magdelena . . ." Her name was a chant on his lips, a canticle to the gods of love for what he had found with her.

"Magdelena?" Another less melodious voice filtered through to her consciousness, the sound coming closer, accompanied by searching footsteps. "Magda-lay-na?"

She uncurled her fingers from their stranglehold on his arms and opened one eye to look at the half-closed bedroom door that would probably pop open any second.

"I should answer that."

"Mmmmmmmmmm." The response was muffled against her neck.

"It's probably Deirdre. I should go find her before she finds us, don't you think?"

"Mmmmmmmmmm."

She could feel him smile and nuzzle closer, cuddling against her warmth. She had given him that, she thought with pleasure. She had endowed him with a contented peace. It felt good. It felt right, and she wasn't the least little bit bothered by the fact that she would have to be the one to preserve their modesty.

"I'll hurry." She slid out from under him and covered his gorgeous nakedness with the sheet. "Don't run away before I get back."

"I'll be lucky if I can crawl before tomorrow morning." He wrapped his arms around the pillow and curled up.

"Men." She pulled her leotard up over slightly shaky legs. "No wonder women are the superior sex. Our necessary systems don't all shut down after making love." She bent down to kiss his nose and exited the room, her face radiant with satisfaction.

"Magdelena?" Deirdre's voice came from the last bedroom she'd cleaned. "Where in heaven's name are you?"

"Here." Magdelena gathered the wet strands of her hair back and tried to braid it into some semblance of order as she hurried into the room.

"Don't tell me you've found your way into the river again." Deirdre set a bag of supplies on the floor and inspected her niece.

"Of course not. I just took a shower after this room. I was all sticky." Well, it was partly true. She peered into the shopping bag of goodies and rifled the contents. "What's this?" She lifted a container out of the bag and held it up to the light.

"It's polyurethane finish for the downstairs wood floors. Bailey and I thought it would be a very good protectant. But, Maggy, I didn't rush back here to discuss varnish. Magdelena, are you listening to me? I have something of the utmost importance to discuss with you, and all you can do is stand there with a ridiculous, silly smile on your face."

"I'm listening. I'm listening." She set the can aside. "For heaven's sake, Deirdre, what's upsetting you?"

"What's upsetting me is that you told me you were planning to buy the lodge from your Mr. Wade." She shook her hands up in frustration. "And now Bailey tells me no, that your Mr. Wade plans to buy the lodge from you, and that he's going to discuss it all with you today. He apparently had Bailey contact several real estate agencies about getting an appraisal done on the property, and he's sent a letter to his attorney requesting that all the proper papers be drawn up."

"He wouldn't." Images of the boathouse and his promise flooded her mind and the smile faded from her lips. "He didn't." She gripped the back of a nearby chair so tightly her knuckles turned white.

"Maggy, my dear, I've just finished telling you that he would and did. What's the matter? Is there something wrong with the acoustics in this lodge? There seems to be a massive lack of communication. Either that or nobody is listening to anybody else."

"Why did Bailey tell you?" It didn't matter, but Maggy needed a few more precious seconds to compose herself.

He said he didn't want me to be spending your money or my money on a project that wasn't yours."

"Over his dead body it isn't mine!" Controlled, gripped finally in an icy calm, she fairly seethed with anger. The hurt at the betrayal was thankfully a secondary emotion.

"You've got steam coming out of your ears, Magdelena Marie. I assume you're not referring to Bailey in your threat?"

"I'm speaking about that insincere, word-twisting, conniving man who's cornered the market on slick moves!" She kicked the water bucket that had been left in the room earlier along with the rest of her cleaning supplies. "What a first-class fool I am! I should have known. I should have suspected something," she mumbled as she began to pace the room. "How in the world could I have imagined that he would give up an entire half of a lodge for someone like me? For someone with all the speed of a snail. All the mental speed, that is."

"Pardon?" Deirdre's head swiveled back and forth like a spectator at a tennis game.

"I'll show him some speedy, slick moves." Grabbing the handle of the bucket, Magdelena hefted it in both hands and ran from the room, dripping dirty water all along the way, a wickedly intent gleam in her angry eyes.

"Magdelena!" Deirdre hurried after her. "You're not going to hit him with that bucket." It wasn't a question. "An assault-and-battery charge will not help you win this case in court."

"I'm not going to hit him with the bucket." She nudged Joshua's bedroom door open with her hip. "I'm not a barbarian, Dee. All I'm going to do is hit him with what's *in* the bucket. Believe me, the shock he's in for is nothing compared to the shock I just received. And a little water isn't going to hurt him. He's not as sweet as sugar. He won't melt."

Swinging her arms back, she took aim and let the cleanser-laden, murky, foul liquid fly, watching with no little satisfaction as the entire mass landed with marksmanlike accuracy squarely in the middle of Joshua Wade's back.

"You realize of course that this means war."

Magdelena took several deep, calming breaths and rocked back on her heels to look up at him. For at least the last half hour since her impetuous act of revenge, she'd been waiting for this, biding her time by cleaning the floor of the downstairs game room, keeping her mind on the eradication of dust and dirt and not on the confrontation that was certain to come, no matter what she did to hide from it. She was only surprised he'd waited this long to confront her.

"We've been at war all along, Mr. Wade," she responded at last, not rising from her kneeling position. "I was just too stupid to realize you were using strategy other than a direct attack." Her eyes were veiled and cold as she looked up at him, her emotionless face giving nothing away to tell him what she might be feeling inside.

His face, on the other hand, was not so closed to her. His eyes were dark and troubled, his strong jawline set stubbornly. The manner in which he carried himself was a classic study in barely suppressed emotion. Towering above her, he wore an almost tangible aura of tension along with the clean clothes and freshly washed hair.

He hadn't come directly from the sneak attack. She probably had Deirdre to thank for her very life. Right now it didn't seem like much to be thankful for.

"I could very happily wring your pretty neck, Maggy." He crouched down to her level since it was obvious she wasn't going to come up to his. "Was it my sexual technique or my inability to stay awake after we made love that drove you to try to drown me in my own bed?"

"This isn't funny." She looked around the clean, bare room she'd just expended her enraged energies on. "And there's no need for you to lie to me anymore. Please." A flicker of something akin to pain flashed across her face, quickly extinguished as she lowered her head, busying her hands and her concentration in opening a gallon can of varnish.

"Was that it?" she asked softly as she bent the bristles of a paintbrush in her fingers, testing their flexibility. She could scarcely breathe, the hot air in her lungs held inside purposely, lest everything else she wanted to demand of him burst forth and bring a flood of tears along with it. "Was that it? Did you tell me that you'd sell me the lodge just to get me into your bed? Or did you take me to bed in the hopes that your admittedly virile prowess could persuade me to change my mind about selling the lodge to you afterward?"

"Neither, damn it!" Grasping her chin, he jerked her head up to meet his gaze and, twisting the paintbrush from her fingers, flung it across the room. "Look at me, Red," he commanded as she dropped her gaze.

It hurt to look at him. She tried doing it without really seeing him, attempting to replace his vivid image with something else in her mind's eye.

"And *listen* to me. Because what I'm about to say will affect us both for the rest of our lives. I'm falling in love with you!" He shook her by the shoulders when she flinched from the words as if he'd struck her. "I think I love you, Maggy. Nothing's happened to change that, wash water included. Nothing you will ever do, nothing you can dream up in that insecure mind of yours, will ever be able to change that. I never once told you that *you* would own the lodge, though I plead guilty to allowing you to think it. I wanted you so badly, and I knew that if you believed it . . ." He dropped his hands from her stiffly held shoulders. "If you'll remember, all I promised was that by the end of the summer we would no longer be business partners. We won't. I will own Whitewater Lodge, all of it, by then. I didn't have to take you to bed to accomplish that. I took you to bed because that's what we both wanted. One thing has nothing to do with the other."

"No?" She smiled bitterly. "Deirdre said you were going to try to persuade me today, but you didn't. How long was the pretense supposed to go on? Until you were sure I'd sell? Until you asked me to marry you maybe and didn't have to buy my share at all?" She laughed deprecatingly as he opened his mouth to speak. "I warn you, I have had some experience in that kind of a courtship."

"Dammit, Maggy! I'm not Wes!" he exploded at her. "I'd planned to tell you today about my intentions, but I decided to wait until Monday when my lawyer had the papers drawn up and a fair assessment of the property made." He looked at her directly. "And maybe I was stalling. I have to admit that I wanted to wait until after the weekend to make you an offer on the lodge, in the hopes that you'd want to stay here with me after the papers were signed."

She rose to fetch the paintbrush from the other side of the room, and dipped it in the varnish. "I'll stay all right!" Varnishing a wide strip of floor, she placed yet another barrier between them. "But I'm not selling Whitewater Lodge to you, Joshua Wade, or to anyone else. Not now, and not at the end of the summer. And I'm not staying on anywhere as a fringe benefit to go along with the property. So if you're not selling out to me, if you're determined to be my business partner, then that's fine with me. All other possibilities and options are canceled now anyway." She varnished another swath of floor and then another, widening the gap between them, creating a glossy no-man's-land that he wouldn't be able to cross.

"Look at the offers before you decide," he said flatly, reaching across the sticky obstacle to hand her three sheets of stationery, each from a different real estate company. "They're rough estimates of Whitewater's worth, based on what the lodge and business were worth three years ago in their heyday, and taking into account current property values. I'll pay you ten percent above the highest estimated market value quoted there, as soon as I can get the lodge back on its feet enough to float a loan of that size."

She snatched the papers from him and spread them out on the floor. "I've looked at them." She wiped at a tear that had somehow squeezed past her guard. "And I'm going to frame them for posterity. Three offers for Whitewater Lodge that I turned down!" Tipping the varnish can slightly, she flooded a large section of the room in polyurethane. "Anytime you're in doubt as to my position, feel free to come in here to remind yourself. But leave me alone!" Spreading the varnish out evenly, she quickly coated the papers and effectively glued them to the floor, covering them and the area around them in sealant.

His expression hardened, but he made no move to touch her again, to reach her again as Deirdre came to stand beside the door. "You haven't won the war, Maggy mine," he promised her in an ominously quiet voice. "I *will* have Whitewater Lodge, and I *will* have you. You might as well resign yourself to those two facts and save us both some grief. I have no intention of letting either of you go."

Deirdre remained in the doorway long after Joshua had gone, watching the furiously flying varnish brush.

"You've painted yourself into quite a corner, Magdelena Marie. Now what are you going to do?"

Squatting Indian style in the remaining three-foot

section of unvarnished floor in the room, Magdelena turned baleful eyes in her aunt's direction, knowing the question held more than the obvious meaning.

"I'm going to crawl out the window and finish painting this last spot from the sill. What else? It's what I planned to do from the start."

Deirdre wasn't one to take a hint that a subject was taboo. "You can't run away from love forever, Magdelena, and then find a convenient escape when things get sticky."

"Please, Dee." She reached for the nearby sill, swung herself onto it, then leaned back to finishing varnishing the last corner. "I'm not up to cute analogies today. What do you want?"

"Only your happiness, my dear. Only that. And it makes me more than just a little frustrated when I see you running away from it without taking a good look at it first."

"You're referring to Joshua's financial offer, I assume?"

Deirdre leaned over to get a better look at the three pieces of paper lying tackily under their coat of varnish. "Whether you sell this piece of property or not is irrelevant," she said, shrugging. "Whether you fight the suspicion and distrust that is your real legacy from Wes or not is very relevant. Wesley Dailey ruined a year and a half of your life. What do you propose to do, let him ruin the rest of your life as well? Because if that's the case, there was no reason for you to get that divorce. You'll never be free of him until you leave behind the way he made you feel."

It was painfully close to the truth. "With Joshua Wade?" Magdelena demanded angrily. "That's hardly a reasonable option, considering everything."

"I had a long talk with him. He's not out to hurt you. Quite the reverse. And even if that weren't true,

Maggy, what happens between you in a business sense has nothing to do with the way he feels or the way you feel. We love whom we love, logical or not, reasonable or not. Sometimes we make poor choices, sometimes lucky. Most people don't throw water at their lucky choices."

"Words of wisdom from an expert on love and romance? I don't see you celebrating a silver wedding anniversary," Magdelena snapped thoughtlessly, biting her waspish tongue seconds too late.

"Some of us weren't lucky enough to fall in love with someone free to return the feeling." Deirdre turned away so that only her profile was visible, her head held proudly erect, still, her eyes unblinking.

"I'm going to glue my tongue to the floor." Maggy offered the soft apology tentatively. "I didn't mean that. I never thought about you and a husband. I always thought you were married to your work. I'm sorry."

"Not as sorry as you could be if you don't give what I have to tell you some serious consideration." Deirdre banished her own regrets for the time being. "You rarely listen to the voice of reason, which is why I rarely attempt to force you to do so. But try to take a piece of very good advice to heart just this one time, my love. Don't wait to let someone into your heart until you think you're safe from feeling any pain; don't run away from involvement just because one relationship didn't pan out. If you do, you may wake up one day to discover that life has passed you by and that there's nothing left for you to do but sit on the sidelines and cheer other runners on."

Magdelena listened to the silence after Deirdre had finished speaking, wondering if her aunt would accept any comfort she had to give, even if she had to walk back through the varnished room and ruin the finish to give it.

"I'm going to be busy with my own law practice for the next couple of weeks," Deirdre said suddenly, her voice as strong as steel chain without any weak links. "But you'll have Bailey here to help you, and Joshua, if you'll let him. By the way, in case I don't see you before Saturday next, I've ordered some new dining room chairs and furniture, Bailey's picking out a good pool table, and you should be receiving applications for a chef, some waitress/busboy types, and a few maids."

Magdelena's jaw hit the floor at about the same time as her brush hit the bottom of the varnish can. "Why are we in such a rush?" Things were moving speedily enough as it was, weren't they? She was getting dizzy just watching herself.

"Didn't I tell you? I placed an advertisement in the papers announcing an open house on the thirteenth, fourteenth, and fifteenth with free food and drinks during the cocktail hour, a live band, and free rafting trips to the first thirty people who reserve one of our ten available rooms on one of the three consecutive opening nights." She chuckled dryly at Magdelena's incredulous gasp and waggled her fingers in farewell. "The two of you are going to have to come to a truce rather quickly or the lodge is going to fall flat on its face."

Seven

"I've never believed anything positive could come of a war before, Magdelena. But after seeing what you've done with this lodge in such a short amount of time, I'm inclined to review my original opinion."

Deirdre did a 360-degree turn inside Magdelena's spacious private room and whistled through the small gap between her front teeth. Spic and span from floor to vaulted ceiling, the bedroom, like all the others upstairs, now boasted new carpeting and drapes in varied autumn colors, highly polished hardwood furniture, and the scent of fresh pine oil.

"You've done a bang-up job, my girl, much better than I thought you'd do, certainly better than you would have done if you and your Joshua had kissed and made up, as I advised. By the way, what have you done with him? When I met Bailey at the front door, he grumbled something about your sending Joshua off on—and I quote—another damned snipe hunt."

"Do you mean to tell me he's not back yet?" Magdelena swore in a very unladylike fashion and clasped a pair of emerald earrings that had once belonged to her mother into her ears. She gave herself a quick once-over in the full-length mirror, not pausing to enjoy the transformation from her usual casual image. Her long coppery gold hair had been swept up and coiled smoothly around her head, her makeup was dark and alluring, and her grass-green silk gown clung tightly to her breasts, waist, and hips, then swirled seductively around her long legs to the tips of her darker green high-heeled sandals.

"He was supposed to be back here hours ago," she continued, glaring at the bedside clock radio that glowed a fluorescent 4:30 P.M. "We're scheduled to open our doors to the public in half an hour and half the management team is out snipe-hunting. Great. Just wonderful! I'll make him eat those stupid flowers a petal at a time."

"Flowers *and* snipes?" Deirdre followed as Maggy raced out of the bedroom and down the stairs to the first floor. "Something exotic to serve along with Bailey's Hopi venison chili and adobe bread?"

Magdelena groaned and ran from room to room, hoping against hope that Joshua would have had more sense than to leave her alone at a time like this, all in the name of making a good impression. She wasn't up to facing their grand opening alone!

"Bailey!" she bellowed, hitching her skirts up to a manageable midcalf level, and rustled her way into the recreation room where Bailey spent a good portion of his free time.

"Where is he?" she demanded of the room's lone pool player, whose one concession to their big day, a clean white T-shirt, was being rapidly baptized in cue chalk and whiskey from their well-stocked bar.

"On a quest," he said, studying the table.

"I know that." Lord save her from bullheaded, close-mouthed men! "What I don't know is where, and what I have to do to bribe you to go out and drag him back by his . . ." She thought better of it. ". . . by his nose if need be."

"He didn't exactly say where he was off to." He tapped a pool cue on a side pocket and proceeded to knock the orange ball off the table entirely, irritably befouling the air with puffs of cigar smoke in response.

"What is going on here?" Deirdre asked him as Magdelena raced out of the game room to make sure everything else was ready for the open house.

"Ask yon trouble bird." Bailey puffed the cigar discontentedly. "Ever since she dumped the water dish on their love nest, we've had nothing but squabbling and ruffled feathers around here. If Josh isn't flying around like a gooney bird, working us both to death trying to forget that his little lovebird exists, he's strutting his feathers like a demented peacock and doing everything short of flying south to get back in her good graces. Right now he's off somewhere in the canyon looking for wildflowers to put on her dining room tables. Wildflowers!"

He started to add more to the story, but another, louder outpouring of discontent reached their ears, coming from somewhere at the back of the lodge.

"You are certifiably insane!" Magdelena said to Joshua as she removed his slightly squashed backpack. She led him from the back door to the stairs, picking up the flowers that dropped from him as he moved. "Only a crazy man would climb a sheer rock face, freehand, for heaven's sake, to pick some stupid flowers that are only going to die anyway by morning. You're lucky we won't be using them for your funeral. And, in case you hadn't noticed, I'm not impressed. Everybody under the sun for miles around will be coming to see how well we run the lodge, and the owner is going to greet them all at the door wearing orange globe mallows in his hair." She picked at the delicate bright orange petals that were clinging to his blond hair. "And then I suppose you plan to sit down to dinner with all those tuxedos and suits surrounding you, wearing a mud-stained sweatshirt, filthy running shoes that look like you've been mucking around in rabbit droppings, and grubby jeans covered with—ahhh!" She shook her fingers in the air. "—with cactus spines. Oh, that's the icing on the cake!" She motioned him upstairs, taking pains not to come into direct contact with any part of him again. "I don't suppose you'd care to enlighten me about how you managed to cover yourself with cactus spines?"

"I would." He lifted his legs carefully and ascended the stairs. "I will as soon as I defoliate myself. My clothes aren't the only things covered with sprouting spines. And incidentally, without a hand mirror and double joints I'm not going to be able to work too quickly, so you're going to have to sit down to dinner alone. I'm afraid my sitting-down days are over for a while."

"You're not doing this to me," she warned as he reached his bedroom. "I'm sending Bailey up here to help you . . . with your problem." She managed a sympathetic groan as he gingerly pulled his shirt up, exposing the cactus spines that dotted his spine.

He dropped the shirt onto the bathroom floor and twisted like a pretzel to see his back in the bathroom mirror. "Bailey and I are friends, Red, but I think it would strain the bonds of friendship and my dignity to ask him to take cactus needles out of my butt." He rummaged through the bathroom drawers, looking for a hand mirror. "This is something I'm going to have to cope with alone, just as you're going to have to cope with the opening alone."

"How did you get cactus needles there?" She wasn't

going to get through this evening without extremely frazzled nerves. "You weren't flower-gathering in the altogether, were you? I mean, thrill-seeking is one thing, but . . ."

"Don't be ridiculous." He reached one arm up and back, trying to reach that difficult spot just under his shoulder blades. "My clothes were on. But even I can't climb and hold onto a handful of flowers at the same time. After I'd filled the backpack, I saw a clump on a ledge just above my head that were perfect." He gave up on the cactus spines irritating his back, and pulled his boots and socks off, using only one hand to do the job, his other held conspicuously out and away from his body. "I had put the flowers in the back of my pants when I lost my footing and fell, right into a bed of cactus I hadn't noticed growing underneath the ledge. When I reached around to pull what was left of your bouquet out of my britches, I realized, unfortunately a little late, that I'd used one hand to break my fall, and it was covered with needles. Hence my problem."

She smothered an exasperated snort. "I'm going to find Deirdre. Stay here." There was only one thing to do and she was going to need some help. "You're not going to be able to take care of this alone."

"Magdelena!" he yelled. "You are *not* bringing Deirdre in here to de-needle my backside!"

She laughed at the thought and covered her lips to hide a smile. She wasn't planning any such thing. But it would satisfy her frustrated lust for revenge if he thought she was. "I'll hurry back. Don't run away."

"The last time you said something like that I had to sleep on the floor for a week while my mattress dried out on the front lawn," he growled irritably. "And I don't like the idea of anyone else knowing about this. I feel lousy enough as it is."

"Bye." She slipped out the door and closed it behind her, leaving him to stew in his own juice, as it were, while she went to find help. Taking the stairs at breakneck speed, she spied just the help she needed.

"Wait just a minute!" she called out to Bailey, who was on his way to sample the hors d'oeuvres before the rest of the guests arrived. As she reached the first floor, she even managed to corner Deirdre, who was discretely eavesdropping at the bottom of the stairs. "I need your help. We're going to play Queen for a Day here, and you've both just been promoted to resident royalty. How would you like to be the stand-in owners and greet our guests as they come in?" She didn't wait for any probable negative answers. "Good! I knew I could count on you!" She glanced up at the ornate sunburst clock that filled the wall over the main desk. "It's four forty-five now. At five P.M. sharp you open the doors. Let everyone in and show them around downstairs. Make sure everyone's supplied with whatever they need, and if I'm not back down by the time the chef says soup's on, make sure everybody gets enough to eat." She took a deep breath and mentally crossed things to be done off the list. "The band is due to arrive here an hour after we open the doors, and about a half hour into the dinner." She swung Joshua's pack up from the floor and deposited it in Bailey's astonished arms. "Speaking of dinner, find somebody to put these on the dining room tables. There are agave and ocotillo blooms, globe mallows and—"

"Cactus thorns!" Bailey dropped the pack and cursed loudly.

"I'm sorry," she said contritely, starting back upstairs. "And cactus thorns, which are what I have to spend the grand opening of Whitewater Lodge pulling out of my co-owner's derriere."

She took the steps two at a time, leaving Bailey

gaping open-mouthed and Deirdre with a smug smile of satisfaction on her Cupid's face.

"I'm back," she called, giving Joshua advance notice before pushing the door open.

"Alone? And without a bucket of wash water?" a suspicious voice said from behind the bathroom door.

"Yes to both counts." She closed the door behind her. "I left the mayor and his wife outside, along with that reporter from the Phoenix newspaper, a representative from a local travel agency, and half a dozen assorted guests and hangers-on. But I'm making no promises on how long Deirdre and Bailey are going to be willing to keep them occupied, so . . ." She admonished herself for a disgusting lack of courage. What could the man do with the lower half of his body incapacitated? ". . . so let's quit stalling. Drop your pants and let's have a look at you," she said quickly, struggling to keep her feelings from showing.

There was total silence from the bathroom for a few moments until the sound of a zipper broke the stillness, the sound of metal against metal mingling with the sound of someone hyperventilating.

Was it she? Or Joshua?

"Oh Lord, Maggy mine . . ." Joshua stood before her outside the bathroom door, stepping slowly out of the blue jeans, his completely nude body silhouetted in the dim light. "I've wanted to hear you say something like that for so long."

Magdelena swallowed with some difficulty. "On second thought, maybe you'd better put a robe or something on and let me take a look at your hands first."

"Already de-needled, while you were gone." He advanced on her like a lithe wildcat, wearing his nakedness naturally, proudly. "You'll have to look at the rest of me, whether you like it or not."

Whether she liked it or not? He was either being

facetious or the fall he'd taken onto the cactus had scrambled his memory. It hadn't erased hers. She could still vividly recall each centimeter of him, the taste, the smell, the feel of him.

"I'm here to look at your cactus spines, Joshua, which don't seem to be bothering you half as much as you led me to believe. I'm not here to look at anything else." Her voice had risen to a nervous high squeak.

He handed her a pair of tweezers and, purposely brushing her body as he passed, lay face down on the bed. "Is your vision problem the kind that makes things look bigger or smaller than they really are?"

"My vision isn't that bad!" she informed him testily, and turned the bedside lamp up high. The firmly muscled length of him was bathed in light, the thin white strip of bare skin usually covered by his shorts drawing her attention in spite of her vows to be objective. How in the world was she going to look at him closely enough to remove cactus spines without really getting close enough to see him? How was she going to touch him without really feeling him, feeling all that he made her feel?

"I'm not great at being able to see fine details," she warned him breathlessly. "I'm going to need to get fairly close. So if you feel me breathing down your back, don't get any ideas."

He sighed contentedly as she sat down next to him on the bed and leaned over his naked body. "I'm afraid the ideas are already there. However, if you insist, I'll do my best to keep them on a tight leash."

"I insist." Keeping a watchful eye on him, she placed her hands on his back and worked from the top down, plucking cactus splinters along the way and doing her best to accomplish the task without giving thought to anything else.

"If I had known a few cactus spines and a little

discomfort were the key to such nirvana," Joshua mumbled, "I'd have impaled myself on them a long time ago." He reached back with his hand to stroke her legs.

"Will you stop? You promised." She held the pair of tweezers away from him. "You're making me shake and I'm missing them."

"You're making *me* shake. And I only said I'd do my best. You're making it very difficult."

"Try harder." She pulled her legs in closer to the bed, away from his grabby reach, and resumed her search-and-rescue operation on his back. "Joshua!" She smacked his industriously seeking fingers with the tweezers. "If you don't hold absolutely still, I'm going to have to use restraints."

"Kinky."

"Yes. Particularly since the restraints I was thinking of are Deirdre and Bailey. Maybe they can convince you to hold still. On the other hand, maybe we should just move the party upstairs. We could use your bed as a table and keep you as the centerpiece, using these rather pointy spines to skewer cherry tomatoes and fresh mushrooms and cubes of cheese." She slipped away from his momentarily still hands, using the time to search for further unseen barbs, stroking his back up and down carefully, feeling for any more. "It's hard enough finding the little devils without having to extract them from a moving target too."

"Sorry." He walked his fingers contritely back to his side of the bed. "I can't help myself. My hands seem to have a mind of their own where you're concerned." He rolled a little to one side, exposing more than a glimpse of the front of his body. "So does the rest of me. Couldn't you just leave the others to work themselves out and take care of my more chronic problem, Florence Nightingale?"

She tore her eyes away from the sight, tormented by the thought of his chronic problem, and the way he was using it to melt her resolve. "If I don't get all the needles out, they're going to get infected. Do you want that to happen?"

"That depends on whether you'll agree to kiss them and make them better."

"Joshua, don't." She was finished with the spines on his back. The ones in his buttocks were all that remained. "This is difficult enough as it is."

"You ought to try it from my end . . . no pun intended." He laughed. "You have me at several distinct disadvantages, not the least of which is that instrument of torture in your hands, and the fact that I can't roll over and take advantage of the first time you've been near my bed in weeks." He ground his teeth as she quickly finished the job with less than her previous consideration to his tender skin.

She took a deep breath and rested her hands against his back to keep her fingers from shaking. The sole way she'd been able to maintain a business-only relationship with him, with both of them living in the same lodge, had been by working eighteen-hour days and staying as far away from him as possible. Her anger at him for the way he had maneuvered her into his bed hadn't kept her from wanting him. Knowing the wisdom of keeping things on a strictly business level hadn't either. Neither had her fear of loving and losing again. Telling herself over and over that a friend and partner of Wes Dailey's was no one to fall in love with still hadn't been enough to keep her from needing him, from wanting to walk down the hall and open the door to the paradise she knew he would share with her.

She leaned down and rested her head against the small of his back, grateful that he was in no position to see the aching desire on her face. She was through with her reason for being there. There was no reason to stay with him now, here in the quiet of his room. There was every reason to leave, including the mayor and his wife who, though they hadn't actually been downstairs before, were very probably down there now, waiting none too patiently for their hosts to put in an appearance.

"We should go." Was she the only one with a conscience? she wondered.

"If you're looking to me for strength of character in a decision I don't agree with in the first place, don't. Nothing's changed for me. Say the word, Red, and I'll lock that door, unplug my telephone, and say the hell with the party."

"You wouldn't." They'd worked so hard on this, he every bit as much as she.

Easing gracefully off the bed, he crossed the room in a few short strides and locked the door. He turned back to her, holding his arms out, his eyes burning with a fierce desire and an even stronger hope. He had answered her challenge and issued one of his own.

She stared at him dumbstruck, knowing that unless she found a way out of his room now, she'd never make it. She wouldn't be able to think of a single reason important enough to keep her from knowing his possessive embrace, if just for a brief moment.

"I have to go!" She pushed herself up from his bed like a sleepwalker, fully intending to walk past him and out the door . . . until she walked into his arms instead. Only then did she come to life, soft silk against hard, naked muscle, melting the space between them with the heat of a passion no longer held on that tight leash. A cry of release tore from her throat, its meaning not lost on him, although she hadn't uttered a single intelligible word.

"It's been hell for me too, Maggy," he murmured, stroking her hair gently. "Lord, I've missed you so very, very much these last weeks." Moving his hands down over the form-fitting gown, he caressed her with a mixture of tenderness and lust. "You look like a forest nymph in that dress. You *feel* like a combination of every sensual fantasy and erotic daydream I've ever had the pleasure of experiencing. It doesn't feel like you're wearing a stitch underneath . . ." He drew several ragged breaths and ran his fingers slowly down the silky lines of the gown. ". . . it doesn't feel like it, but you are, aren't you? You wouldn't entertain half the town with nothing on underneath your gown . . ."

She had no intention of pouring gasoline over an already out-of-control forest fire by admitting that underwear would only spoil the gown's sleek lines. "I'm admitting nothing. You're only guessing."

"You've kept me guessing since the moment we met."

"The feeling's mutual." She tilted her head back, giving up the battle, and kissed the tip of his chin. That was all she could conveniently reach until he groaned and brought his mouth down against hers, fierce need winning out over tenderness.

His mouth moving over her lips as if to memorize the feel of her, he pulled her in closer to his demanding desire, his hands rifling through the carefully arranged hair, stroking the hollow of her cheeks. Dropping his hands to her breasts, he tugged at both taut nipples at once, persuading them to stiff peaks of desire that pushed against the silk gown.

"Every man who sees you tonight is going to want to book a night in our lodge in one of our rooms . . . yours. Sweet Magdelena, tell me how I'm supposed to concentrate on making a good impression on the mayor and his frumpy wife when all I'll be able to do is think about the feel of your breasts in my hands, and the touch of your hands on the part of me I'd most like to pin you to my bed with?"

Listening to his voice and the things he said, which were eating away at what remained of her resolve, she hadn't been aware that her hands were undertaking a sensual journey of their own, rubbing, circling, massaging his body until she approached the hard thrust of him.

"Touch me, Maggy," he begged as she drew her hands away in confusion. "Touch me, please. Don't be afraid. I won't do anything but stand here. I'll take root right here if you'll only . . . mmmmmmmmmm."

She gave in to the pressure of his will and the pressure of her own conscienceless needs with a shudder that shook her entire body. Her lips parted and her eyes were brilliantly bright as she watched him and his responses to her caress. He was all smooth, rounded muscle, rigid with wanting, engorged with the same blood that pounded loudly in her own ears. Stopping, standing still, was the farthest thing from her mind. She wanted him to move . . . within her!

"Stop!" He closed his fist around her hand, his fingers unknowingly biting into her skin, a muscle twitching at the side of his face. "I won't force you, Magdelena, but I can't take much more of this. If you go any farther, I'm not going to be able to let you leave me tonight, even if it means chaining you to my bed and ruining my previously unblemished reputation." He slowly released her hand. "Stay with me tonight, Maggy. Don't make me sleep alone again, not tonight, not when I feel the love you still have for me." He brushed his lips against hers, willing her to speak the words he wanted to hear.

She licked her lips. The need to spend the night wrapped in the warm cocoon of his passion was warring with the fear of waking up in the morning once the narcotic of her own desire had worn off. She could only give herself to him so many times before there would be no turning back. And she wasn't ready for that yet.

"What are we supposed to do with our lodge full of guests? Tell them to go home and then expect them to come back later when it suits us?" She offered the perfectly valid argument, knowing, as he did, that it had nothing to do with the real reason she was pulling back from him.

He let go of her reluctantly and unlocked his bedroom door with a loud click. "I'm not giving you up." He didn't pretend to believe her excuse. "It's only a matter of time." He smoothed the wayward strands of her hair back from her troubled face. "I'm just conceding that this isn't the right time for the kind of lovemaking I have in mind." He opened the door and gently pushed her through the opening. "Go now. Please. Before I change my mind and do something for which our accountant, financial backer, and managerial consultant would shoot me at sunrise."

"Right." Maybe he had a conscience after all, she thought with a half smile, or at least some business sense. "I'll tell them you're coming. They're probably all chomping at the bit."

Her first thought, as she descended the stairs to the sound of laughter and lots of conversation, was that if she turned around very slowly and went back up, no one would be the wiser.

The mayor *was* chomping—on a thickly sauced barbecue rib, leaning against the bottom of the stairwell amid more people than she'd known existed in the whole of Arizona.

Spilling out of a tightly packed dining room, they were carrying plates of food and balancing drinks on whatever flat surface presented itself, surging from one place to another in a tide of noisy, chattering humanity.

"Magdelena! There you are, dear." Deirdre motioned her over to a minuscule open space near the bottom of the stairs. "The mayor and I were wondering when you'd find us in the crowd. But I should have known you'd be upstairs with the help, seeing to a few last-minute details. So conscientious."

Magdelena grimaced inwardly. There went her last chance to escape. "Sorry I'm late." Taking direction from Deirdre's comic behind-the-back gestures and none too subtle nuances, she apologized to the small group of people who seemed to be clumped loosely around a man whose photograph regularly made the local papers. "I'm afraid I had a bit of business to attend to. I'm Magdelena Dailey, half owner of Whitewater Lodge." Extending her hand to the mayor and his wife, she nodded cordially to the others in the group, acknowledging introductions and doing her best to place names with faces for later recall.

One of the people she'd been introduced to, a handsomely dressed man who represented a local travel agency, moved to stand on the step just above her.

"Bob Banks," he re-introduced himself. "I think that's quite admirable, attending to business on your opening night when you're obviously dressed for a party." His light-brown eyes rested warmly on the soft shimmering folds of her dress and the curves displayed, discreetly now, underneath.

"My niece has been very attentive to the business end of things lately." Deirdre's face remained amazingly blank even as Magdelena choked on the reminder of where she'd been for the past forty-five minutes.

"That's all the more reason for her to take some time off now to enjoy herself." Bob casually dropped one hand to the small of her back. "And since I do believe I hear the band starting up, I'd like to be the first one to help her celebrate this grand opening with a dance. Magdelena?"

She fidgeted uncomfortably, looking for an excuse not to go. How was she going to get out of this one? "I should try to mingle with my other guests too, get to know some of the people . . ."

"No problem." He wasn't about to take no for an answer. "I'm Arizona Travel's local branch manager and I know nearly everyone here on a first-name basis. I'll introduce you."

"Swell." Magdelena shot an imploring look to Deirdre, who had suddenly struck up an involved conversation with the mayor's surprised-looking wife. "You will find me if you need me for anything, won't you, Deirdre?"

"Absolutely." Her aunt smiled innocently. "If I need you I'll send someone to find you. Enjoy yourself." Deirdre grinned impishly, a mischievous gleam twinkling in her eyes.

"Thanks." Maggy bit her tongue to hold back a more sarcastic retort and let Bob guide her through the throng of people and out onto the dance floor. What was the matter with her? She was only going to dance with a good-looking, successful man who appeared to have been instantly attracted to her. There was no reason to treat him as though he were a consolation prize rather than the sweepstakes grand prize. She allowed him to hold her loosely as they began dancing to a slow melody. It wasn't his fault that he wasn't an appealing six-foot-three-inch tawny blond giant with flowers in his hair and thorns in his fanny. She smiled at the mental image and laughed softly.

"Did I say something funny, or are you laughing at my obvious lack of dancing skill?" Bob asked.

"Neither, and I apologize for making you think anything of the kind. I was just thinking of my first reaction when I came downstairs and saw all these people. If it had been possible, I think I would have turned tail and run. We advertised the grand opening quite heavily, but I never dreamed we'd get this many people. I'm not complaining, mind you, and I did expect the lodge to be packed during the summer season. We *are* a resort lodge. But I had no idea there were so many people looking for a place to dance and have a bite to eat on a Saturday night in the winter."

"You'd be surprised." He seemed ready to launch into a favorite subject. "America's on the move. I could give you statistics . . ." He smiled reassuringly. "But I won't. I left the office behind, other than to keep an open mind about whether this was the sort of place I'd recommend to clients. And weren't you supposed to leave the office behind too?"

"I will, after you tell me what your recommendation is."

His gaze rested on her appreciatively, his arms moving her almost imperceptibly closer. "If I had any sense at all, I'd tell everybody it was a terrible place with worse food and no atmosphere. That way I could hope to have a few quiet dinners here with you all to myself, without half the town as an audience." He looked around the room, raising his hand in a half wave as a couple beside them greeted him and danced by. "But I don't think it would do any good. From the looks of things, half the town already knows what a special place you've made this. The only thing they don't know is why it's so special." He paused deliberately. "You're what makes it special."

"Bob . . ." She had to let him know that she wasn't interested.

"Come on," he said as he straightened, obviously not wanting to hear anything that started out with a regretful "Bob . . ." "You did want to meet some of your guests, didn't you?"

She looked around the room, filled with people who doubtless knew her gregarious dancing partner and who would, if he had any say in the matter, believe them to be an item by tomorrow morning. Could she escape him gracefully?

"I did want to meet some of the guests," she improvised. "But frankly I'd rather let it go for another evening, if you don't mind." She tried to let him down gently. "I'm having enough trouble remembering all the names to go with the faces as it is. Any more and I'll end up calling all the Toms Bill, or worse, Mary. And I hadn't noticed it before, but I've discovered that I'm mildly claustrophobic. Right now I'd just like to get some air and a bit of space."

"That's an even better idea. It would take most of the evening to introduce you to everyone I know anyway. It would be easier to just point out the few people here I don't know."

"Like me, for example," a deadly calm voice said quietly, the tone conveying far more than the words could imply.

Magdelena's head snapped up instantly as Joshua insinuated himself into their conversation and onto their small dancing space, crowding ever closer until the three of them appeared to be dancing a new trio step.

"I'm Joshua Wade, half owner of this lodge," he said to Bob. "It was good of you to keep my partner company while I was otherwise occupied. Thank you." If he had physically picked the man up and set him aside, his intent could have been no clearer.

"It was a pleasure." Either Bob wasn't willing to see the wisdom of relinquishing her, or he wasn't quite as intelligent as she'd previously given him credit for being.

"What do you want?" Magdelena asked Joshua point-blank.

"Deirdre said you were looking for me," he admitted. "I assume there's been some mix-up in communications. However, now that I am here, I'm sure there's *something* we need to do as the host and hostess."

"I was hoping I could persuade our hostess to show me around the grounds," Bob interjected. "I'll need to have some idea of the lay of the land, so to speak, if I'm to represent it well to my clients."

Touché. She had to give him credit for a quick response to Joshua's needling. "I think that's a good idea," Magdelena said, trying to smooth things over. She took his arm and turned to make a quick exit off the dance floor.

"*I* have a better idea." Joshua put an arm around Bob's far smaller shoulders in comradely fashion. "Why don't you plan to pay us a visit early next week? I'll make it a point to show you around the grounds myself. You seem to be a man who likes to live dangerously. Maybe you'd like to take a short river trip on one of our rafts? It can be quite exciting, easily something to tell your clients about for a long time to come." Leading Bob off, bulldozing a path through the dancers, Joshua left Magdelena alone on the crowded dance floor to wonder if and when he would return to abscond with any future partners.

She wasn't going to stand for this! She zigzagged her way to the French doors that led to the outside. She wasn't going to let Joshua run her life like that. She was a businesswoman, and Bob a potential client.

"I don't know where you think you're going." Joshua's large hand closed over her upper arm and drew her outside. "But you're not going after him."

She whirled on him, glad that they were alone on the patio and out of earshot of the majority of their guests. "As it happens, I'm not going after him," she said angrily. "I was coming to look for you."

"That's more like—" he started to say.

"But not for the reason you think," she added, struggling to keep her voice down. "I want to know what you did with him."

"Your travel agent took an unscheduled trip home."

"You threw him out?" She couldn't have heard him correctly.

"I persuaded him there was no valid reason for him to stay."

"He was a perfectly nice man!" She was fairly shaking with rage. "You had no right to do that!"

"I have every right!" he thundered. "And he was a very lucky man, lucky I didn't toss him head first into the river the way he was pawing all over you, and you without a stitch on under that damned dress." He jerked her into his arms, his hands tightening possessively around her ribs.

"Dance with me, Red," he said at last. "They say music soothes the savage beast. Don't you want to see me soothed?"

"I don't know what I want." She let him hold her, moving slowly and out of sync with the music, more confused than she could remember being at any other time in her life.

The lead singer's voice filtered out to them and Joshua picked up a few lines of the song, singing them to her in a low baritone.

"I don't want to need you, but I do. I'm afraid to love you, but it's too late. It's true. In my heart, in my life, there is only room for you . . . for you . . . for you . . ."

The music continued but Joshua's song for her alone had ceased, actions replacing words. He stroked her back to caress the thinly covered curve of her hips, his fingers kneading the sensitive nerve points at the bottom of her spine with a deep sensual pressure. Their hips and thighs moved together in a natural, rhythmic harmony possible only between lovers.

Magdelena tightened her hold around his shoulders and neck, hiding from the rest of the world, burying her face in his chest. Her breathing quickened to match his, her senses heightened by all the raw emotion.

"I couldn't stand the sight of you in another man's arms," he confessed. "I couldn't stand wondering if you were thinking about having a relationship with him. The thought of him holding you like this, touching you like this, the thought of that damned traveling-salesman type knowing your body like I do . . ." He shook his head as if to clear it. "It was driving me over the edge. You're mine, Maggy. And I have no intention of letting any other man have you, even if it means evicting off the property everyone in pants over fifteen and under sixty."

"No!" She twisted away from him, not willing to be seduced by her own need for him any longer. "We are business partners, Mr. Wade, who happen to feel a certain amount of physical chemistry. That's what it is. And it's not something we have to give in to. My personal life is—as I want it to be—none of your damned business!"

"Like hell it isn't!" He stalked her as she paced the small patio. "You belong to me, Maggy." His conviction held the strength of cold steel.

"I'm not a piece of real estate for you to buy shares in. I don't belong to you on the basis of . . . of one regrettable weekend. In case you hadn't noticed, I don't need your blessings on my private life. I'm over twenty-one and I'm a free woman."

"Then I envy you!" he shouted. "Because I haven't been able to free myself of you since you came hurtling down the river and washed into my life. If you want to know the truth, I've given up hope of ever being free of you again. I'm in love with you." His voice was raw. "And if I don't find some way to convince you that you feel the same way about me, it's going to destroy me."

Eight

The sounds of the party within trickled through her consciousness again. She was alone. The patio garden had that solitary feeling, though she hadn't yet summoned up the courage to turn around and check that theory. Bracing herself, she opened her eyes, grateful that her instincts had been correct for once. She was alone on the patio—and in her room at night, and to all intents and purposes, in the lodge . . . in her life. Alone. She wrapped her arms around herself, suddenly chilled in spite of the night's fairly mild temperature.

A young couple with their arms entwined burst out of the French doors, their laughter forcing her to pull herself together. She didn't have the time for a bout of self-pity. She had a lodge to run, guests to entertain, and business to see to. That would have to be enough.

"Magdelena?" Deirdre stopped her with a concerned look as she came back inside and passed the main desk. "Are you okay?"

Was it that obvious? She feigned a momentary

puzzlement. "Okay? Of course I'm okay, Deirdre. Just busy." She hurried on by, not sure she could stand up to Deirdre's lengthy scrutiny. She hadn't lied. She'd simply chosen to redefine. As in Obviously Kicked in the Teeth, or Over-Killed with passionate male emotion, or Obsessedly Krazy to continue feeling this way about a man she'd already decided not to have a relationship with. She flashed Bailey a thumbs-up sign and a reassuring smile as he went to speak to Deirdre, just in case he'd formed the same opinion that she was not okay. Clearly she was going to have to wear her heart somewhere other than on her sleeve, she thought tiredly.

The rest of the night passed in a thankfully numb blur, the Magdelena Dailey she thought she'd left behind in Chicago surfacing to her rescue. She smiled, talked, and went about her business as if this night was as trouble-free as her expression indicated. She chatted with the guests who had booked rooms for the night, gave an interview for the newspaper, listened to a local historian's account of the lodge's history, played pool with a group of teenagers who'd come with their parents, and in general flitted from group to group, being as perfect a hostess as Joshua was a host . . . always at opposite ends of the lodge.

"Did you think they'd ever go home?" Deirdre was perched on the edge of a dining room table several hours later, sipping a cup of strong tea as Magdelena supervised the cleanup crew.

"I didn't think any of them remembered they had homes, or jobs, or children to tuck into bed, or anywhere else to be but here, or anything else to do but party until sunrise." Magdelena leaned wearily against the same table.

"It's not quite that late," Deirdre guessed. "It can't be more than three A.M., because when Joshua and I poured the last one into a cab for home, it wasn't quite two-thirty."

"That's going to cost him a pretty penny back to town." Magdelena brushed bread crumbs from the table onto the floor for the carpet-sweeper to take care of.

"It would, but you're picking up the tab." Deirdre drained her teacup. "He insisted on paying for his drinks with five-dollar bills while Bailey was manning the bar, and then refusing the change. Bailey was sure we made a good fifty-dollar profit on him alone. I figured we owed him a safe ride home. You know, speaking of profit, in spite of my generosity and your free drinks and hors d'oeuvres during the cocktail hour, you made quite a handsome sum of money here this evening. I have never seen so many hungry and thirsty people all in one place with so much money to spend. I thought the chef was going to faint. As it was, he had to send out for more food twice."

"You think that's good?" Magdelena raised her voice to be heard over the sweeper. "All that's left in Bailey's well-stocked bar are a few bottles of that Russian vodka that went unopened in some sort of political protest, and the dregs of a quart jar of maraschino cherries." She surveyed the dining room when the sweeper was turned off.

"How about we call it a day?" she said to the exhausted cleanup crew who had gathered to await further instructions. She smiled at their weary chorus of affirmative responses. "And what about you?" She tilted her head back to lean against Deirdre's shoulder. "You're not going back to town after the night you put in. The least I can do is offer to share my room for the night and make you one hell of a big breakfast in the morning. How about it?"

"I appreciate that." Deirdre picked up her teacup and deposited it on an empty wheeled cart that was being pushed into the kitchen. "But I have a date with a bottle of twelve-year-old Scotch and a deck of cards."

"A what?" Magdelena raised her eyebrows in surprise.

"A date with a bottle of *pilfered* twelve-year-old Scotch, my payment for this evening's slave labor, and a deck of cards. I have every intention of beating the pants off that old river rat in poker and drinking him under the table before morning."

"Who?" Magdelena gaped openly, looking as if she had just discovered her original Picasso masterpiece was really a kindergarten finger-painting.

"Bailey, of course. Who else? I finally found something that he and I have in common. We're both insomniacs. I'll be out in the boathouse if you need me." She paused meaningfully. "I trust you won't need me, Magdelena."

"Bailey?" This was going to take a few moments to digest. "Bailey?"

"You only go around once in life, my dear."

Bailey? Magdelena walked out to the main lobby, still puzzling over the unexpected bit of information as the cashier turned over the day's receipts and money.

"Thanks, Clara," she said. "I'm going to lock up now. Are you driving home alone?" The older woman lived by herself and rarely went out in the evening. She'd made an exception for the grand opening.

"Yes, ma'am, but I'll be fine. It's good of you to be concerned."

Magdelena smiled and locked the cash and checks in the floor safe. "I have selfish motives. You're irreplaceable, especially at your pittance of a wage." She handed Clara her coat and purse from behind the desk. "Be sure and call if you need anything." The phone rings in my room at night, and that's where I'm headed now."

"Oh . . ." Clara held a hand to her mouth. "I forgot to give you a message. Mr. Wade said to tell you that there's a problem with your room and that you need to speak with him before you go upstairs."

"He did, did he?" She bit her lip and gave Clara a grateful nod. "Umm, thanks for giving me the message." It wouldn't do to confuse the employees or to put them in the middle of a fight between two bosses.

"A problem with my room, indeed." She locked the front doors and snapped the lights off, finding her way upstairs by memory and the light of the moon that filtered in through the windows. The only "problem" with her room, in his mind, would be that it wasn't his. Reaching her bedroom door she turned the knob first one way and then the other, frowning as the door remained stubbornly closed and locked in spite of her rattling. Had she gone to the wrong room in the dark? She lifted her eyes to check the number, only then seeing the square piece of white paper taped just above eye level.

"M: Your room's been rented for the night. Come see me for the details. J." She read the message aloud, as if verbalizing it could clarify its meaning. Rented her room? *Who* had rented her room?

Summoning up as much irate energy as she could muster at three in the morning, she marched down the thickly carpeted hallway. Partner or no partner, emotional upheavals or not, he wasn't going to get away with doing this to her. He had no right to rent her room out to somebody. If he'd felt the need to rent out anyone's room, he should have rented out his own. She raised her fist to pound on his door loud enough to wake the dead, stopping just as her fingers were about to make contact with the wood. Why hadn't he rented his own room rather than hers? He'd bunked with Bailey in the boathouse before. Surely it would have been more logical for him to give up a room than for her.

She lowered her fist slowly, scowling blackly at the door. He'd expected her to come storming into his room, all of her concentration directed toward him. Moreover, he'd wanted her to come. He knew only too well how close passionate anger was to passionate desire, and how much harder it would be for her to keep the two separated in the privacy of his bedroom. Knowing it didn't help. If she barged into his room to tell him just what she thought of his sneaky tactics, she was honest enough to admit that he'd more than likely end up with more than a piece of her mind. On the other hand, she wasn't going to get any satisfaction whatsoever by pretending he hadn't thrown down the gauntlet and then spending the night curled up on the lobby benches.

Tiptoeing slowly back downstairs, she reached the lobby phone and dialed his room number.

"Hello, Red." He answered on the first ring without waiting to see who it was. Who else was it likely to be at three in the morning? "I wondered when you'd get around to calling me. You've been up to your room, I take it?"

"No." She injected a hopefully believable dose of curiosity into her voice. "Should I have been? Clara just told me you wanted to speak to me. She didn't say you wanted to speak to me in my room."

"I didn't. She didn't say anything else?"

"No." She was getting better at this, she decided. "In fact, she told me just as I was on my way out to play some cards with Deirdre and Bailey. I'm too keyed up to sleep. I only called because I thought it might be important." Sometimes she surprised herself with flashes of pure, unadulterated genius.

"It was only important if you wanted to spend the night in your room. That's what I wanted to talk to you about. Deirdre and I found one of the guests weaving from room to room, drinking the dregs of everyone else's drinks. No I.D., no one around to tell us who he was or where he lived, and he didn't remember. I know it's an imposition, but I couldn't very well send him home in a cab if I didn't have the address to send him to. So I thought . . ."

"Don't worry about it. I understand." She did, too. It was suddenly all very clear to her as she remembered Deirdre's earlier comment. *When I helped Joshua pour the last one in a cab . . .* There wasn't anyone in her room! Joshua had invented the entire thing, believing that she'd have to come to him for details, and that he could then persuade her to share his room since there was "someone" in hers, someone who would be mysteriously gone in the morning when she woke up.

"Maggy?" His voice sounded curious over the phone. "Are you still there?"

"Not for long. I'm going out, so I'll see you in the morning."

"Maggy, wait." There was a modicum of honesty mixed with the urgency in his voice. "I need to see you. I left a note on your bedroom door. I was hoping you'd come by to talk to me after you read it. It's important that we talk."

She wound the telephone cord around her hands, closing her ears to the aching need she could hear in his voice, not lost over the wire. She couldn't go. If she did, the decision to give in to his persuasive "talk" would be out of her hands. She needed time alone to rebuild her defenses. She heard his deep intake of breath as he realized she either could not or would not give him an answer.

"One of these days you're going to get tired of running, and you're going to have to face this."

She held the phone in her hand a long time after the small click at the other end indicated that he'd hung up. She was tired of running *now*, so tired . . . so very . . . very . . . tired. . . . Her head nodded forward once, twice, her eyelids weighing heavily over gritty, lackluster eyes. This was not a time to be making crucial decisions. This was a time for a long hot shower and the peaceful nonexistence of sleep.

Trudging upstairs, she knocked softly on her own door, and when there was no answer, unlocked it with a passkey and went in. The room was empty, as expected, the warning knock only a precaution.

She stripped the silk gown over her head and tossed it onto the bed on her way to the shower, belting a satiny pink robe around her waist as she walked. A *short* hot shower and then to bed. She'd had enough for one day. One more problem, one more dilemma and she was going to—

"Araggggghhhh!" She gripped the bathroom doorway for support and stared down at the room's occupant with suddenly wide-awake eyes.

Looking a bit like a tubby department-store Santa Claus minus his red velvet suit, the tipsy middle-aged elf who was grinning at her from inside the shower stall didn't need anything further to make him jolly. His round, well-padded body was clothed in a three-piece suit that reeked of gin and tonic and looked like it belonged in an advertisement for a stain-fighting detergent. His hair was skewed every which way and falling down into eyes that were undoubtedly seeing double and triple images of her.

"What are you doing in my bathroom?" She forgot for a moment that she *had* been warned, and that he looked in no shape to give her a coherent answer.

"Waz gonna take a shower," the inebriated Santa's helper slurred. "But the water-turner-onners are too high to reach. See?" He lifted one pudgy hand to prove the point and let it drop back down to cover his face. "I don't wanna shower anyway now. I wanna go to bed. Not feeling any too good." He reached clumsily up to hit a fist against his chest and missed the mark, slamming it into the shower door instead. "Bad ticker, ya know."

"Oh, great scott!" She moaned in unison with her uninvited guest, a two-part harmony of mutual misery. "Come on." She bent down to get her hands under his armpits. "Let's get you out of the shower and into bed where you'll feel better." She tugged at him with enormous effort and very little success. "Never let it be said that Whitewater Lodge was inhospitable to its guests." She scrambled out of the way as he struggled to his feet. He swayed like a palm tree in a hurricane as she guided him out of the bathroom and toward the bed.

"Just a few more feet, my friend. Come on, buddy, you can make it." Walking backward, she coaxed him on with all the precision of a traffic cop directing a truckload of fragile eggs over a potholed roadway.

"You're a nice lady." He had to stop to speak, incapable of doing two things at one time. "What nice lady are you?"

"The one whose bed you're going to be sleeping in."

"Oh." He stopped again. "I don't think my wife's gonna like this."

"She'll like it." She coaxed him forward again with a reassuring nod. "I'm *not* going to be in the bed with you. Now, come on before I forget what a nice lady I am and what a hospitable innkeeper I'm supposed to be and let you sleep it off on the floor instead."

He tilted his head down, his body following until he jerked it back upright again, his sloppy bulk teetering back and forth. "The floor?" He looked way over to see his feet, which was a big mistake.

"No! No! No! Not the floor! The bed!" Lunging forward to grab him as he toppled, she did her best to keep at least one of their four feet underneath them. It was a dismal failure. She watched in horror as he stepped and swayed and leaned and finally pitched forward until all of his weight was being supported by her woefully inadequate arms. With a dual cry of pain and surprise, they flopped back onto the bed, his heavy body on top of hers, his chin striking the top of her head as they hit.

"Help." She lifted one of his totally limp arms from her throat and squeaked a plea, trying to roll out from under him or push him off her or wake him up long enough to get him to help her do one of the above. It didn't take long for her to realize none of those plans were going to work. The situation had escalated to an unmanageable level that required immediate, if unpleasant, outside intervention. She struggled to reach the bedside telephone that was thankfully within reach of her free arms, and dialed a familiar in-house number.

"Whitewater Lodge." The greeting was sleepy and none too welcoming.

Tough! "This is room number three, down the hall." She added a nasal twang to her voice. "I have a *large* problem with my bed and I want to see the manager about it immediately." She waited the several seconds it took for him to remember that room number three was hers.

"Maggy, do you know what time it is?" He sounded somewhat less than pleased to hear from her.

"I'm in no position to see the clock." She tried to wiggle out from under her hefty cover again and failed.

"I'm in no mood for practical jokes," he warned her. "Maggy?"

Her laughter was slightly hysterical.

"Maggy?" He paused. "Magdelena? Where are you?"

"In my bed," she answered sweetly. "And I'm not alone." She hung up the telephone and resigned herself to wait the amount of time she calculated it would take him to reach her. Ten, nine, eight, seven, six, five, four—

Joshua burst into the room wearing a ridiculous-looking long-sleeved red nightshirt that left his muscular legs mostly bare. "Maggy!" he yelled. "Are you all ri—" His worried question fell away unfinished, his concerned eyes crinkling at the corners in ill-concealed laughter.

"Maybe I should go back out and come in again after you've had time to compose yourself?" He bowed. "Pardon, madame, for catching you and your corpulent cohabitor *in flagrante delicto.*"

"I'll *flagrante delicto* you, you practical joker, you conniving . . . oohhh!" She clawed the bed in a renewed effort to free herself. "Compose myself? You walk in here looking like some sort of a hairy overgrown tomato and you tell *me* to compose myself?" Her eyes raked over his attire, her expression saying it all.

"I'll have you know this is quite warm. I sleep in it occasionally when I'm forced by circumstance to sleep alone. Not all of us are blessed with such a *big* source of cheap body heat. If my appearance offends though, I'll be happy to take myself back off to bed and see you in the morning."

"You do that—" She gasped for a full lung of air. "—you do that, you leave me pinned underneath this blubbery land shark all night long, and I swear you'll never be able to close your eyes again without wondering what I'm going to do for revenge. You'll never know a peaceful moment! You'll need a full-time bodyguard!"

He stopped and closed her bedroom door, no longer leaving, but not in a big hurry to relieve her of her cumbersome bed warmer either. "Land shark?" He shook his head. "It looks more like a beached whale to me. Though of course beauty *is* in the eye of the beholder. What did you call me in here for, Maggy? Am I to save you from a fate worse than death? Or was that a coy invitation to join *a ménage à trois*?"

"*Ménage à . . . ? Get me out of here!* I'm into one-on-one relationships, thank you, but this one is going to squash the life out of me if he stays on much longer."

"I can see that." Squatting down next to the bed, he nudged her sleeping land shark's still body. "Not a very vigorous lover, is he?"

"Joshua, please." If he wasn't going to get her out of this, she was going to have to renew her efforts to do it herself. Flailing about, she dislodged the nearby pillows, the phone, and part of the coverlet, but not the one thing that counted. "My kingdom for a lever or a stick of dynamite or—" She stopped to listen to Joshua's choking laughter. Tears were running from his eyes and down his cheeks. Ohhh! If she could only get her hands on him! "You're responsible for this. I want him off my body and out of my bed. Now!"

"That could be difficult." He stifled the laughter, except for an occasional chuckle, and circled her bed thoughtfully, his amused eyes never leaving the behemoth sprawled on top of her. "He must weigh well over three hundred pounds if he weighs an ounce. Maybe I'd better call the fire department rescue squad."

She could see it all now. "You do and I'll never, never speak to you again."

"I didn't think we were speaking to each other now," he said musingly. "Since you appear to have changed your mind on that score though, why don't you tell me how this happened? Practice your story for the press while I think of a way to describe your predicament to the fire department."

"The press?" Her head popped up from the bedspread in alarm. "What story to the press? We can't tell the press about this." She peered at him anxiously, her head swiveling from side to side as he paced from one end of the bed to the other.

"Don't you remember?" He raised an eyebrow in surprise. "That reporter from the paper reserved a room next to yours for the night. We'll hardly be able to smuggle a crane in here without him hearing and coming out to ask questions and take pictures for the paper."

"Don't do this to me, Joshua," she begged, already imagining the front-page headlines and accompanying photos. "The publicity will be as terrible for you as for me."

"Worse," he said glumly. "Do you have any idea how it's going to affect my reputation, let alone my sense of self-worth, when word gets around that you preferred to go to bed with him instead of me?" He slapped his hand against her bed companion's shoulder. "I'd hate to admit publicly that *this* was the better man."

"And he said he had a bad ticker," she said, suddenly remembering. "What if something's happened to him? Everybody will think he died while he and I were . . ."

"You're a real heartbreaker, Maggy. But then I've always known that."

"And you're awfully chipper, all things considered, Dr. Jekyll." She glowered at his lack of support. "Tell me, what did you do with Mr. Hyde?"

"Banished him from the house along with your travel agent, neither one being worthy of you," he assured her seriously. "And I'll get you out, without any publicity whatsoever, if you'll do just one tiny favor for me."

"Name it." She was in no position to negotiate.

He sat down on the bed next to her. "Give me a chance to redeem myself. We need to talk. I need to apologize, and I'd like to do it tonight. Come back to my room with me." He met her suspicious eyes with a solemn, level gaze. "Nothing is going to happen that you don't want to happen, Maggy. I promise you that. I'll stay on the other side of the room if that's what you want me to do. And whenever you want to leave, the door will be open . . . and un-guarded. Deal?"

There was really very little choice. "Deal." She held her hand out to him. "Now, who are we going to swear to secrecy to help you get this miniature space shuttle off of yours truly?"

Cracking his knuckles for the effect, he bent over theatrically, like Hercules about to wrestle with a ferocious bear, and, wrapping his arms most of the way around the unconscious man's middle, lifted him up and off her, depositing him gently onto the floor. Straightening up, he held his hand out to her in a gentlemanly fashion. "Shall we go and leave him to believe you were just a very real and delicious dream?"

She took his arm, feeling a little as if she was in the middle of a dream herself, one that she had no control over. She was exactly where he had wanted her to be in the beginning—on her way to his room—and moreover, feeling an uncomfortable gratitude instead of anger.

Waiting for him to close the door to his room behind them, she chose a spot to defend, as far away from him and the invitation of his bed as she could get, knowing even as she did so that he could shatter her defenses with a touch.

"Maggy, I—" He began speaking with his back to her, stopping short as he turned and saw her protective stance.

She was leaning against the wall nearest the door, her fingers curled defensively around her upper arms. Her eyes were wide with uncertainty, watching his every move, her face haunted with fatigue and a desire she didn't want to be feeling.

"My God, Maggy! What am I doing to you?" He walked to her in two quick strides and gathered her stiff body into his arms, then carried her to the bed, pulling the blankets back before laying her down.

She stared at him as he extracted two more blankets from his closet and brought them back to the bed. This was it. This was what she had been aching for for weeks, what she had been dreading for weeks: the touch of his hands on her body, the feel of his mouth on her skin, the heady intrusion as he poured himself into her. He was the personification of every erotic fantasy she had ever had, the knight in shining armor she'd dreamed of as a girl, the passionate lover she'd yearned for but never had as a bride. He was the kind of man she'd always envied other women for finding: sensitive, caring, intelligent, funny, and maybe just a little possessive. He was here, standing before her, and she didn't have the courage to reach out for what her body and her soul were begging her to take. Loving him and losing him would decimate her life as Wes hadn't been able to do. Loving him was a risk she couldn't choose to take.

But the choosing and the taking were out of her hands. They were in his, and it was too late to run away now. He eased himself into the bed alongside her and reached over to brush her upswept hair, his fingers drawn there as to a fire on a cold winter's day.

"You know we can't go on like this, don't you?" he said hoarsely. "I want you more than I've ever wanted anything in my entire life. I can't continue to live under the same roof with you and not have you, not have some hope of having you."

"I know." She could anticipate his next move, could feel the need in him reaching out to her.

He pulled her closer until their bodies met, her body pressed intimately against the length of his virile desire, the silky satin of her robe and the thin cotton of his nightshirt all that kept them from what they both needed. He held her painfully close for a few brief seconds, savoring the feel of her. Then he rolled over and placed the two extra blankets between them as a barrier. She felt alone and terribly, terribly confused as he turned onto his side, his back to her. He spoke at last, his voice low with an underlying sadness.

"I can't stay here at the lodge with you anymore. I think that's become obvious to both of us. It's intolerable for me, and for you. For reasons I don't care to share with you right now, I cannot sell my half of Whitewater. But I can put Bailey in charge and go back to Colorado. The company I used to work for wasn't happy with my leave of absence in the first place. And I have it on good authority that they'd turn handsprings if I'd agree to return on a permanent basis. I can't promise we'll never meet again, Maggy, but I can leave your everyday life in peace. Maybe if I'm several states away I'll be able to find some peace of my own again."

An icy wave of cold and guilt swept over her, threatening to drown her with its crushing weight. She could feel the intensity of his pain even though his back was hunched over, away from her in an attempt to keep that pain all to himself. He wouldn't let her see it, let alone share it. He was saying good-bye, shutting her out of his life.

Feeling a loneliness that was as devastating as it would be enduring, she reached across the barrier to touch his tightly clenched hand, his rigid shoulder. "Joshua?"

"Don't say anything," he said, the words clipped, bitten off precisely to prevent any more vulnerable emotion or sound from slipping through. "Just get some sleep. You need it. Trust me, I know how you feel and I won't transgress anymore. I'll start making the arrangements to get out of your life in the morning."

He was going to do it, she realized. He was going to let her live without knowing any emotional encumbrances or risks. And all she had to do to ensure that secure cocoon of safety was agree that his decision was what she wanted, strike the blow that would confirm his intentions, eradicate any small hope that might remain in the depths of his heart that there could be a future for them.

She parted her lips to say the words and exhaled raggedly, the words sticking in her throat. If only he hadn't told her he was going to do it. If only he had just gone and given her no choice or chance to make him stay. If only he hadn't been so painfully sure she would agree with him. If only she hadn't heard the resignation in his tone, and if only he hadn't cared enough to sacrifice his own needs for hers. If only . . . if only . . . Then she could have let him go, found the words to agree with him, and said good-bye. But it would have been a lie. She would have been living a lie. She knew it in the depths of her heart, even if he didn't. And inexplicably, the risks of letting him stay and assume some role in her life were less painful than the cold, solitary certainty of what would happen to her if she let him go.

She tentatively touched his leg, feeling a freedom that was as exhilarating as it was frightening. He had been right; Deirdre had been right. You couldn't run away from love forever, not without trampling all over the things that mattered most in the process. She climbed out of her side of the bed, intending to circumvent the blanket fortress he'd surrounded himself with.

"Magdelena?" he asked. "Where are you going now? If you still don't feel comfortable with me here, I can always go bunk with Bailey and let you sleep here alone."

She eased into his side of the bed and pulled the covers up to their necks. "I have a feeling Deirdre wouldn't like that, and, as much as she deserves to be interrupted in revenge for similar past injustices, I don't want to see you leave." She found his leg in the darkness again and moved her hands up, outlining his calf and knee under the blankets. Stroking his hair-roughened thigh, she continued in her upward journey until she reached the smooth expanse of his hip, the powerful warmth of his male core.

"Maggy, I don't know what you think you're doing,

but I don't need or want a physical demonstration of your pity or your gratitude." He tensed under her touch and pulled the nightshirt down to break the forbidden contact, reaching back to reposition the extra blankets between them.

She laughed softly in the darkness. "I write thank-you notes to people I feel grateful to and I write tax-deductible checks to people I pity. I don't make love to people in either group." She took the blankets back and dropped them over the side of the bed, out of his reach.

"I put those there for a purpose," he snapped.

"I know you did." She played with his hands that were holding the nightshirt down. "Double-wide, thermal wool chastity blankets. But we don't need them anymore. The Pennsylvania Dutch might have used bundling to prevent any unwanted hanky-panky in the beds . . ." She threw back the blankets that covered them and unbuttoned the top two buttons of his night shirt. ". . . but this isn't Pennsylvania, and I think it's a little late to prevent us from experiencing the joys of the flesh, don't you?"

"I think I'm confused." He prevented her fingers from exposing any more of the skin at his chest.

"Then let me clarify things for you." Pushing herself up to a sitting position on the bed, she unclipped the barretts holding her hair up and shook the curls loose, letting the dark red cloud frame her face and shoulders in a halo of softness. Slowly loosening the pink satin belt at her waist, she let her robe gape open, the soft roundness of her breasts revealed as she bent over him to finish unbuttoning the nightshirt, her fingers sure and certain.

He caught and held her hands midbutton and crushed them to his chest. "People who play with fire, Red, almost always get burned. It's an old cliché but it's quite true."

She drummed her captive fingers against the well-developed muscles of his chest, which was moist with a slight sheen of perspiration. He fairly glowed with an inner heat that she was responsible for starting, and she longed to share the warmth of that blaze.

"It's too late," she said. "I'm a victim of spontaneous combustion, so you might just as well get close and take advantage of the heat."

"Are you absolutely sure about this?" he felt obligated to ask. "I'm not sure I'm going to have the control to stop once I start."

"That's good, because I don't want you to stop."

The words had scarcely left her mouth when he took the proffered advantage, closing the small distance between them until there was no distance. His mouth prevented further speech, his tongue was a thrusting, moving point of pleasure, starting waves of hot quivering sensation wherever it touched.

It touched everywhere, starting with the blue-veined pulse point at her temple and working its way around the velvety soft hollow behind her ears, to the heartbeat at the side of her graceful neck, to the juncture of her wrists as she reached up to encircle his face with her hands.

She grinned at him wickedly, daringly, her reservations thrown aside with the blankets. "Are you warm enough now to take off your pretty fire-engine-red jammies?"

A slow smile spread across a suddenly boyish face. "Take them off and see for yourself. Just don't leave your hands in any one place too long, or they'll get singed."

Taking the dare, she gathered the material of his long sleeves up and pulled his arms out, leaving them free to caress her as she quickly undressed him. "Hold still!" she commanded, caught up in her own urgency. "Anyone would think you're trying to fight this."

"Not me." He lay perfectly still as she lifted the garment up and over his head, brushing her naked breasts against his face in the process. "I gave up fighting this a half hour after I met you."

The nightshirt fluttered to the floor, forgotten as he cupped the heavy fullness of her breasts, pressing them together to allow his greedy tongue ready access to both nipples at once.

She melted slowly against him, an ice-cream cone on a hot summer day, her muscles in his power, as he dropped moist, moving kisses around the dark areola and down to the underside of each breast until he reached the delicate strength of her ribcage.

She moaned and arched her body nearer to him, her feminine sensuality urging him on as he lowered her onto the bed and followed her down, his mouth never leaving her skin.

"Joshua!" She cried his name out pleadingly, and curled her fingers in the shining blond of his hair as he circled her navel, charting a spiraling quest downward. "Please! I need you."

"Tell me what you need," he whispered onto her skin.

She sucked in a delirious breath, unable to form the words as his mouth found the joining point of her pelvis and inner thigh. She could imagine what she wanted, could almost feel what she wanted, but to say it aloud? Admitting to everything she wanted from him, having the power to command, rather than being simply swept away on the crest of his passion, was a frightening notion. It meant trusting him. It implied a conscious, thought-out decision to give herself to him and take from him. And once the words were out, she wouldn't be able to pretend that she had let him love her passively. He would know and she would know that she had asked for it, had all but demanded it of him.

She pressed her lips together as he actively worked on short-circuiting her fears and inhibitions, his lips tasting the sweetness of her femininity, his hands holding her still, keeping her where he wanted her to be.

"Tell me what you need from me," he repeated imploringly.

"Damn it, Joshua, I left my *Joy of Sex* back in Chicago. You can't convince me that you really need an instruction manual to know what pleases a woman."

He broke off the tantalizing contact to voice a single, husky promise. "I'm not trying to please just any woman. Any woman would respond in a certain predetermined way if I did certain predetermined things. And I'm not trying just to please. That's too insipid a goal. I'm trying to make love to you, Maggy mine. Big difference. This is as new for me in a way as it is for you, even though we've made love before. And I'm not moving from this spot until I know exactly how to do a hell of a lot more than just please you."

"You were quite close to doing much more than just pleasing me a few moments ago," she admitted in a small voice. "And you don't need advice from the peanut gallery on technique, just on timing. Your timing for a long, involved conversation is abysmal."

He chuckled and resumed his sensual exploration of her body, slowly pushing her thighs apart until she lay vulnerable to his worshipful embrace. "There, Maggy. You don't need to fight me any more. You don't need to run from my love any more. Just let it happen." Massaging with his fingers up her slender, long legs, over the taut, firm skin of her belly to each breast, he stroked her nipples with thumb and forefinger, driving her toward almost unbearable pleasure.

Her breath was coming in shallow gasps and her fingers gripped his arms for support in anticipation of the whirlpool of need that would suck her under the surface of conscious thought and into a swirling maelstrom of ecstasy. She cried out in desire as he caressed her in a rhythmic pattern of pressure, raggedly inhaling a lungful of air through conscious effort alone, having forgotten how to breathe automatically somewhere along the way.

"I want you." She spoke from a need almost too intense for her to comprehend. "Anything you want to give me, everything you have to give me. I want all of you, as close to me as you can get until every part of me has the essence of you. I want you to be a part of me always."

"That's what I wanted to hear." He groaned in long-awaited satisfaction and came up to kiss her mouth, his demanding maleness seeking the sanctum of her body. He moved his hands around to cup her buttocks, his eyes half closed with anticipation as she encircled him with caressing fingers and guided him home. Even then he held back to savor the moment, taking possession of her in slow stages, entering her a little at a time until she arched her hips to receive the full, satisfying length of him.

"Ohhhhh, Maggy mine . . ." He moaned as she tightened herself around him, waiting for him to set the tempo of their dance. "I think I've died and gone to heaven."

She rotated her hips slowly, letting him draw out and surge back in like an ocean tide. "You're not in heaven yet, my love . . . my sweet love . . ." The words came easily to her now, her position in his arms exalted, secure, supreme. "But you will be soon,

soon." She wrapped herself around him, staying one with him as he rolled over to lie beside her, facing her on the bed, their legs and arms entwined, their lips and noses and tongues touching, their hips moving in perfect harmony as the pace of their love-making increased.

He gave a deep gutteral sound and urged her on with a wordless language as old as humankind it-self, until she was matching his deep, piercing thrusts with an equal fervor, until their bodies simultaneously exploded in a supernova of all-consuming passion.

Nine

"You're sure you know what you're doing?" Bailey said, stalking Magdelena as she zigzagged around him from the refrigerator to the butcher-block countertop and back again, extracting cheese and celery and individual cartons of orange juice.

"Of course I know what I'm doing." She deliberately chose to misunderstand him. "I'll have you know that I've packed picnic baskets lots of times. It's easy. All you have to remember is to keep the hot stuff warm, the cold stuff cool, keep the mayonnaise out of the sun, and bring along a fly swatter and extra food for the ants. What could be easier?" She dropped a handful of napkins and some plastic utensils into the wicker picnic basket. "Let's see . . ." She inspected the neatly arranged contents. "Southern fried chicken, Greek olives, German potato salad, French bread, and last but not least, a very good bottle of California Chablis. Chilled, of course. That should be a varied enough menu, geographically, even for a travel agent."

She scooped up the cheese and celery and orange

juice from the counter and put them in with the rest, tilting her head in question at Bailey's thundercloud of an expression. "What's the matter? Don't you think he'll like my offerings?"

Bailey leaned against the counter, his heavy square hands fiddling with the hamper's wooden handles. "That depends on who the *he* is you're talking about, and what you're offering him."

"Oh, let her go and stop borrowing trouble," Deirdre said, then began huskily singing a dirty ditty of World War II vintage. "You didn't pack all of the Anjou pears, did you, Magdelena?"

"Nope. I didn't pack a one. Bob doesn't like them."

"Good. I was thinking I could pack a picnic lunch and go out to the lagoon for the afternoon . . ." She dropped a meaningful look in Bailey's direction. ". . . that is, if I could persuade somebody to ferry me and my grub there in his boat."

Bailey dropped the handles of the picnic hamper and covered his mouth in a sudden coughing fit.

Maggy winked at Deirdre in a silent thank-you. Deirdre was always inventive when it came to devising ways to change the line of questioning. "The lagoon?" Magdelena asked Bailey innocently. "Isn't that the place you two go skinny-dipping?"

"The very place," Deirdre answered for him. "How 'bout it, pops? Are you up for a picnic and a romp in the lagoon?"

"If it's a picnic you're after, he said gruffly, "then we ought to go with trouble bird here and her 'date.' She's packed enough food there for an army."

Deirdre bit into a ripe Anjou pear, retrieved from beneath a pile of oranges in a bowl on the countertop. "I did have more of a private lunch in mind."

Magdelena swung the basket up and over her arm, doing her best to keep her smile under some semblance of control. Lady Cupid had obviously sat down on one of her own arrows, she thought.

"I'll be taking the boat out to do a little fishing 'long about ten-thirty." Bailey gave no indication he'd interpreted Deirdre's blatant message. "I can take you wherever you want to go then."

"Last of a dying breed," Deirdre said, looking far away for a moment after Bailey had left. An expression of girlish wonder replaced some of the usual cynicism. "Do you know, Maggy, I never thought I'd find someone like him at my age. He has the most endearing, gentlemanly way of—" She stopped, keeping whatever the small bit of information was to herself. "*Is* this a date with Bob?"

Magdelena set the heavy basket back down for a moment, its contents weighing as heavily as her conscience. "No," she said firmly. "It's purely business, and I mean that, Dee. Bob's made up a copy of a travel brochure featuring Whitewater Lodge that he'd like me to see. If I like it, I can get it printed up and he'll distribute it to his clients, and help me to get it distributed elsewhere. I realize we're three quarters of the way through our rafting season, but there's always next year to think of in this business, and that's the only thing I am thinking of: business. It just seemed nicer to conduct it over a picnic. Don't I deserve an afternoon off every now and again too?"

"Did I say you didn't?" Deirdre shrugged eloquently. "There's no real reason you couldn't have a nonbusiness lunch with Bob if you wanted to, is there?"

"You're leading the witness, counselor," Maggy snapped. "Just for the record, you're right. There isn't any real reason why I couldn't go out on a date with Bob or anybody else if that's what I wanted to do. I don't have a ring on my finger." She lifted her bare left hand to emphasize the point. "And I've made no commitments."

"Who are you trying to convince, me? Yourself? Or that hunk of a man upstairs that you're not the least bit committed to even though you've worn a threadbare path in the carpet between your two rooms and saved on the linen service by rarely sleeping in separate beds?"

Magdelena bowed her head and leaned it against the basket handle. "Sometimes I feel as though I'm being swallowed by the river again, like I'm caught in the current with no way to get out even if I wanted to."

"And you don't want to, do you?"

"No. Suicidal, isn't it?" She laughed hollowly. "In the almost five months we've been together he's told me more about himself than I learned about Wes in a year and a half, and he's asked me questions about myself that *I* didn't have ready answers for, but that he seemed to know. I've never met a man I was so physically attracted to, and I know he feels the same way . . ." A supremely contented glow lightened her features just for a moment. "We've had fun this summer, even with all the work of rebuilding the lodge and the business, and we've been so very, very close. But in all this time he's never told me it's forever, and he's never asked me . . ." She shied away from the words. "The only thing he has asked me a great deal lately is if I won't reconsider and sell him my half of the lodge. He says he can arrange the financing now that we've had a good season and the business is a proven money-maker." She shrugged disparagingly. "There are times I get the impression he's courting the lodge, not me, and that's an insecurity I haven't felt since that first day when I found out he didn't intend to sell the lodge to me." She lifted the picnic basket again. "Silly of me, isn't it?"

"Unquestionably," Deirdre reassured her. "If he made goo-goo eyes at me the way he does at you, you'd have a run for your money, my girl." She winked and began rummaging in the refrigerator, tossing whatever was in front into a brown paper bag for her lunch rendezvous. "As it is, *I* get to picnic with a slightly paunchy, slightly balding river rat who cheats at poker and can drink *me* under the table. You just don't make the most of your advantages. You don't even realize you *have* advantages! You realize of course that youth is wasted on the young? If I knew what I know now and was in your shoes, my girl, I can tell you I wouldn't be going on a business lunch with Bob. I'd be seducing the man I wanted to marry."

"I don't—"

"Don't lie to me, Magdelena. The temperature goes up ten degrees every time he's in the same room with you."

"That's what I'm afraid of." Her luminous eyes darkened. "When it's over, how will I ever get warm again?"

The sound of a honking horn in the drive chased the darkness away. She brightened considerably, a genuine smile lifting the corners of her mouth. "That'll be Bob. It would be nice if I *could* fall for him, Dee. It would make things a lot easier in the time A.J."

"A.J.?"

"After Joshua." She tugged the heavy basket outside into the circular driveway where Joshua had Bob cornered.

"Magdelena! Hi." Bob reached to take the basket from her.

"Was that you honking?" she asked as he deposited the heavily laden basket in the back of his Chevy sedan, only daring to look up at Joshua after Bob's eyes were averted from her face.

"Chalk it up to exuberance." Bob straightened and cast a furtive glance at the real reason he hadn't been able to get to the door to fetch her properly.

Joshua was dressed in a formidable black wet suit that did nothing to hide his far superior physique. He stood slightly away from the car, his legs braced apart, his black, wet-suited arms crossed over his chest. His expression was veiled, his mood hidden.

"I . . . ah . . . I haven't been on a picnic in years." Bob sought to fill the silence.

"Neither have I." Magdelena chose to ignore it altogether. "That's why I decided to mix business with pleasure today. I even have a place to go all picked out."

"Oh?" Joshua intervened. "Going to the lagoon?"

He seemed only mildly interested. Still, Magdelena thought she could detect just a hint of steel in his question. His eyes were cold and unblinking. "Not this time." She wasn't going to press her luck, but it couldn't hurt to give him something to think about, could it? "I thought we'd go over to that shady spot on the other side of the river where the wild grapes are?" She wished she hadn't put a lilt at the end of that sentence. It wasn't as if she was asking him for permission to go.

"It's a nice place," he agreed politely. "I might see you there. That's my midpoint in the two-hour raft run. It gives the first-timers a chance to see if they want to continue, and it gives the experienced river runners a place to have lunch before we begin the second leg of the trip, which is rougher. You might want to take some pictures of the spot to put in your brochure."

"I might. Thanks." Bob looked at Maggy with puzzled surprise. His encounters with Joshua in the past had not been half so pleasant or nearly so helpful.

"Anytime." Joshua tapped his hand on the hood of the Chevy in farewell. "Gotta go. It looks like my water babies are ready for their swim." He sauntered off toward a car full of budding river rafters, all noisily eager to experience the white water.

"So how's the season going?" Bob asked, attempting to draw Magdelena's wandering attention back to himself.

"Pretty good." She reluctantly tore her eyes away from Joshua's retreating back, trying not to think about the bikinied nymphette who'd latched onto his arm as if he were her own personal life jacket. "The first few weeks had their ups and downs until we got used to things, but we've worked out a very practical system. We've hired a pilot and guide to do the three-day trips, and another pilot and guide to do the day trips. Joshua and a guide do the two-hour morning trips, and Bailey and his partner take them in the afternoon."

"And what about you?" He helped her into the car. "Aren't you addicted to the rush of white water and all that goes with it?"

She assumed a pained expression as he pulled out of the drive and headed out according to her directions. "Not if, by all that goes with it, you mean skinned knees, nausea, near drowning, and a hundred-and-twenty-five-dollar optometrist's bill for a new pair of contact lenses." She pointed to a side road coming up on the left. "Turn here. There you go. As a river innkeeper and raft owner, I'll deny it if I see it anywhere in the brochure, but just between you me and the fence posts, my first and only experience with the river will undoubtedly be my last."

"You're serious?"

"Believe me. It would take a herd of wild horses to get me in another boat on that river again."

"You want me to *what*?" Magdelena sat cross-legged on the picnic blanket, a half-eaten chicken leg still held in her hand, an expression of incredulous shock erasing all the morning's hard-won contentment.

Joshua, who was at this moment supposed to be coming down the river with a raft-load of tourists, was standing on the blanket, dripping river water onto the French bread.

"I said . . ." He panted, out of breath. "I said I need you to come downriver with me. The guide we hired to help with the passengers called in sick, and I can't take a raft of that size down the Colorado alone without someone else to help me keep an eye on the passengers while I keep my eyes on the rocks. Now, I've left everyone back up at the lodge to have coffee and doughnuts, but if we don't get back there and on the river pronto, we're going to have a large group of dissatisfied customers, and a bad reputation for efficiency. And we're going to have to return quite a tidy sum of cash. So let's go." He reached down for her arm to hurry her along.

"Wait a minute! Just hold your horses." She held her hands down to her sides, away from him and his impulsive, unreasonable determination. "We *do* employ other pilots and crew, do we not? Why don't you draft one of them to go along on your suicide mission?"

He uttered an exasperated sound. "I can't, and they're not suicide missions and you're going to have to present a calmer image or you're going to scare half of our paying customers away. Look, our three-day pilot and his crew left yesterday, our one-day team pulled out early this morning, Bailey and his man have a run scheduled for this afternoon, and of our two part-timers, one is waiting for his wife to have a baby that was due two days ago and the other is out of town. So you're drafted, baby, and that's final. Come on."

"I can't crew a river raft." She moved off the blanket, but not up.

"You have no choice." Gathering the four corners of the blanket together, he lifted her picnic lunch up over his shoulder and apologized to Bob, who had been watching without comment since Joshua had dripped his way up to them. "Sorry to spoil your business lunch, but this really can't be helped."

"I understand." Bob helped her up from the ground. "I'll take her back in the car and we can meet you at the lodge."

"Not necessary." Joshua wedged himself in between them. "The speedboat I came down in to look for you will be much quicker."

"You don't understand," Magdelena said. Was she talking to a wall? "This is me, remember? The one who's been known to turn green in water bumpier than a Jacuzzi, the one who throws up on her life jackets, the one who can't see a hand in front of her face after a dump in the river washes her contact lenses downstream. I'm not going to inspire much confidence with my head over the side. What do you expect—"

"I expect you to help me run this business," he said curtly. "If you can't handle that, then I'd suggest you seriously consider my offer to buy your share of the business."

She glared daggers at him. He *would* have to put it that way. "All right already!" She grabbed her picnic bundle from him. "Lead on, Macduff. I have but one favor to ask of you after we get in the raft."

"Yes?"

"Let me sit behind you. If I throw up on anybody, it might as well be the person responsible for making me sick in the first place." She stomped after him and flounced into the speedboat, apologizing to Bob as Joshua jumped in without a further word and started the motor.

"I'm really sorry for abandoning you here," she said. "It's a lousy way to end our picnic lunch, most of which you didn't get to sample. If I had any other choice, I wouldn't do it."

"I know you wouldn't." He winked at her. "And don't worry about leaving me here. I'll get back to town . . . just as soon as I find a place to put all these wild horses Joshua evidently brought with him."

"What was that all about?" Joshua demanded once they were under way.

"I told Bob that nothing short of wild horses could drag me into a river raft again."

"I'm flattered." He turned to grin at her quickly before the river called for his full attention again. "I'll let you groom me and give me a good rubdown later."

She snorted, unwilling to forgive him until after she'd made the run and discovered just what he'd let her in for. "You'll be lucky if I don't put you in the barn for the night and make you sleep on a bed of straw!"

"I could use a good roll in the hay."

She wasn't going to dignify that with an answer, turning her attention instead to the shore. Even so, it took several seconds for her mind to register the fact that they were speeding upriver past the lodge, and they weren't stopping.

"You could use a map," she said. "Pardon me, Mr. In-a-hurry-to-get-back-to-the-lodge, but where are we going?"

"To the lagoon." He paused, exececuting a difficult maneuver through a series of shallow rapids. Wouldn't you like to see Bailey and his guide trade places with us and take my run, in the hopes that we can come up with another guide for this afternoon for *his* regular run so you won't have to go?"

"Bailey isn't likely to perform miracles like that for me if we interrupt him and Deirdre." She chewed her lower lip, contemplating what she could possibly bribe Bailey with to extract this particular favor.

Joshua slowed the boat so that their position in the middle of the river was maintained. "Do you want to see if he's there or not?"

"Go on." She motioned him forward. "How much can a case of Scotch, a box of Havana cigars, and the secret to where Deirdre's ticklish cost me?"

He smiled in private triumph and pushed the speedboat onward, jumping the frothy waves, twisting and turning in and out of the rocks with all the determination of a salmon on its way back to spawn, through the narrow-walled channels and around the sandbars that blocked wider passageways until they came to a smooth, quiet section of the river.

"Almost there." He guided them into the "lagoon," which was in reality only a very wide pool of water situated near the actual river's edge, secreted away off the mainstream in one of the abundant side canyons. Constantly fed by the river's current and a waterfall that spilled out from a crack in the cliffs above, the sandy-bottomed pool was edged with vegetation and surrounded by flat rocks that created a natural barrier from the rest of the river.

"I don't see them," she wailed in disappointment, having almost counted on being able to bribe Bailey to trade runs with them.

"I don't, either." He shut the engine down and, gliding into the deep end of the pool, tied the boat to a low overhanging tree branch. "But then, I didn't expect to." Scooping up her jumbled picnic lunch, he trotted over the rocks to a fairly flat one partly shaded by trees.

"Have you been out in the sun too long, or have I been conned?" She teetered unsteadily over the rocks after him. "Why don't you expect to see Bailey here? Didn't you tell me that's why we were coming, to ask him to trade with us?"

"In a manner of speaking." He unsnapped the heavy wet suit at the crotch and began peeling it off, exposing slim black trunks and a naked chest. "If you recall, I said we were going to the lagoon and I asked if you'd like to see Bailey take our run this morning in the hopes we could find a replacement for your prone-to-seasick self this afternoon. I just didn't happen to mention that I already found him here earlier and asked him." He set plastic containers of food out on the blanket. "He should be making the run now, in fact, which gives us a couple of hours free."

She clenched her fists in fury. "Why, of all the nasty things to do! You chased Bob away without even a decent meal!"

"If you noticed a certain urgency, it was only that I wanted to get you away from him before he decided to show you his etchings along with this supposed brochure." He popped the top off a container of olives and tossed a couple into his mouth as she marched up to him.

"That supposed brochure will help our business considerably if it gets into the right hands."

"Mmmmmm." He swallowed the olives, washing them down with a long gulp of her orange juice. "That sounds like a direct quote from Businessman Bob. Are you sure he was talking about getting the brochure into the right hands or getting you into *his* hands?"

He was jealous! she marveled. Commitment or not, he really cared. "The only thing he got his hands on was a chicken leg. I didn't even get to finish mine."

"Then you must be famished." He opened the container of chicken and pulled out a meaty piece. "Here.

Have a breast." Handing it over to her, he searched the container for a piece for himself. "I'm a thigh fanatic myself."

"You're a fanatic, period." She tossed the chicken back at him in a display of frustrated temper, hitting him in the shoulder. "I demand that you take me back to the lodge. My business plans for the afternoon are ruined, my picnic is in shambles, and I can't eat anything with the prospect looming over my head of spending the afternoon on a raft with you feeling nauseated. So just take me home," she pleaded as he flicked crumbs of chicken coating from his chest. "Please. Have a heart."

"I'm not fond of hearts." He shook his head. "Or livers or gizzards or any of the inner delicacies, and I can't find any thighs. Bob probably ate them just to spite me. I'll have to settle for a back." He found one and bit into it hungrily. "And speaking of backs, there's no need to hide out over there as if yours were to the wall. I'll take you home just as soon as you do me one or two teensy favors."

"I'm in no mood to do you any favors." She crossed her arms over her chest and stubbornly remained standing, refusing to be tempted into a more yielding stance simply because he had mastered the fine art of enticement.

"This isn't going to work, Joshua." Her nose twitched as he unscrewed the wide-mouth lid to the thermos of German potato salad and fanned the pungent, mouth-watering aroma of bacon and vinegar and spices her way. "I can stand here until it's time for us to go back to do Bailey's run. You can't force me to have anything to do with a man guilty of kidnapping and misrepresentation and slander and—"

"—torture. Don't forget torture." He bit into a crunchy end of French bread, holding his hand under his chin to catch the crispy bits of toasted bread and Parmesan cheese that crumbled off.

Her eyes followed his hand to his mouth as he lifted the bread for a second bite, her taste buds watering for Parmesan and toast.

"It must be torture for you to watch me eat all of your delicious picnic lunch here in the shade while you're committed to standing at attention for the next two hours way over there." He reached for another carton of frosty orange juice.

She didn't say anything, but moved a little closer to him, out of the sun which had suddenly made her terribly thirsty.

"Of course, we could eliminate the charge of torture if you'd just acquiesce to a few minor concessions," he continued. "If you do, I'll take you back to the lodge, and who knows, if you hurry and comply, you might even get back in time to call Banal Bachelor Bob back and offer him leftovers."

"You're disgusting," she said decisively.

"I was talking about food. What did you think my requests were going to be?" He licked cream cheese out of the middle of crispy stalks of celery.

She decided not to give him any ideas. "What did you have in mind?"

He grinned devilishly and leaned back against the tree that shaded their picnic lunch, his muscles rippling as he lifted his arms up and linked his fingers behind his head. "Nothing terribly compromising. Nothing you haven't done before."

That thought was somehow not very reassuring. "Like what?"

"Like maybe having a bite to eat with me, taking a dip in the lagoon, spending some time here in the quiet, and letting me give you one or two good reasons why spending an afternoon with me is more enjoyable than spending it with Boy Scout Bob."

"And that's all?" An idea formed in the back of her mind. Revenge was going to be very sweet.

"That's all I'll demand," he replied hopefully. "Though if you're inclined to do more . . ."

"You will take me back though, if I do all those things you just said? Promise?" It was pay-back time.

"Promise." Taking a large ripe olive in hand, he nibbled around the pit, sucking the spicy juices into his mouth along with the dark meaty flesh. "That is, unless you change your mind and decide to stay." He held out his hand. "Want to shake on it?"

"No." He had a way of touching her that melted anger, resentment, willpower, and anything not directly related to making love with him. "I think I'll get right down to meeting your requirements for my parole." He desperately needed a lesson. "A bite to eat, you said?" Taking a carrot stick from a plastic container, she bit into it once and swallowed before burying it, pointy side up, in his cream cheese and celery. "A dip in the lagoon, you said?" Wishing she could see his expression without ruining the dramatics, she purposely stepped off the rocky shore into the knee-deep water, shoes, clothes, and all, continuing with nary a break in stride until she was breast-deep in water. Closing her eyes tightly, she ducked her head under the surface and came back up for air. "Consider me dipped." Sloshing her way back to drip on *his* food, she lifted his wrist to count the seconds on his watch until a minute had passed, all the while aware that she had his full attention, his mood changing from smug victory to incredulousness to annoyance and finally to an amused respect.

"I've spent a little quiet time with you." She let his wrist drop. "And now I'm waiting to hear one or two good reasons why spending an afternoon with you is enjoyable before you *take me home!*"

He eased himself up from the picnic blanket and advanced on her dripping person. "Okay."

"You promised to take me home afterwards," she reminded him. "And I'm listening."

"I never said I'd spell my attractions out in words, Magdelena, that you could listen to. I think I'd rather give you a few reasons you could feel." Closing his hands about her arms before she could run away, he brought her close, oblivious to the wet, clinging clothes that separated them.

She was lost. She knew it as soon as he bent his head to kiss the river water from her face, drinking in the taste of her along with the droplets that clung like dew to her nose and eyelashes and cheekbones.

"Stay here with me Maggy, just for the afternoon, until it's time for our run. I've tried, Lord how I've tried, to give you the time and space you needed from me. I've tried to be content with just the feel of you in my arms at night, without thought of tomorrow. But I keep thinking about tomorrow anyway, and what will happen if I never have more of you than I have now. Worse, what will happen if I don't even have this much."

She hadn't considered that he might have insecurities, too. "I'm not going anywhere now." She moved her arms around to link her fingers behind his back. "So why don't we worry about tomorrow later and concentrate instead on why I'd like to spend an afternoon with you rather than Boy Scout Bob?"

He held her tightly for a few moments, expressing his gratitude physically, without words. Patience, Joshua, he ordered himself. She was here, and it was enough for now. "I don't know," he said, relaxing at last, the tension evaporating from him like the water on her clothes. "There are so many reasons why. It could take all afternoon to tell them all." He caressed her lips with his fingertips.

"I have a solution." She stooped to unlace her shoes and peel off her socks. "Why don't you give me a condensed version while my clothes are drying. That way, if we save enough time to locate another guide for your trip. I might be kindly disposed enough to invite you on another picnic tomorrow."

"How about in for a midnight snack tonight?"

"Convince me." Her cold, wet shirt and pants were draped over a bush beside the blanket. "Make this an afternoon I'd want to repeat."

He did, with just a little help from Mother Nature, the afternoon taking on a life and a music all its own. She exprienced it all with a heightened awareness; the sound of water gurgling in the background mixing with the rustle of the wind as it blew through the weeping willows and cottonwoods and tamarisks, the joyous sound of male and female laughter harmonizing with the mating calls of sparrow hawks overhead. She remembered it in cameo snatches, the feel of his hands as he lifted her up to hold her against his chest, the feel of sun-warmed rock against her bare skin as she sunned herself, the unexpected gourmet taste of leftover picnic food when they finally crawled out of the water, famished for nourishment. And the nourishment he gave her then of a different kind, sensual, heady, fulfilling and, though she couldn't explain why, poignant, as if this time could be the last time for them to love.

"What is it?" she asked him. She was lying on the blanket, watching him as he toyed with but did not drink his Chablis.

He set the wine aside untasted. "I'm back to thinking about tomorrow. Tomorrow it'll be six months since I signed Wesley's papers concerning the lodge."

"And that's why you're looking at my expensive Chablis as if it tasted like cheap vinegar?" His expression didn't soften as she'd expected it to. "What's the matter? Is this why you dragged me away from my business lunch? Did we get some bad news? Do we owe Uncle Sam two arms and a leg and my first-born child? No? Somebody's punctured holes in every single one of our rafts and they won't be repaired until tomorrow? No. I suppose that would be bad news, since we'd have to pay to have them repaired." She brushed the hair on his naked arm back and forth lightly, offering him her touch if it would help. "Do you want to tell me about it?"

"The last thing I want to do is tell you about it. What I really want is to—"

"Tell me," she insisted. Kidnapping, torture, and everything else aside, she loved him, and if he needed her, she wanted to be there to help. She snuggled closer to him.

"Oh, Maggy mine . . ." He suddenly poured out the emotions that had forced him to muscle his way into her day. "All I really want is to see your beautiful face shining with love for me. I want to hear you call my name in the middle of the night in your dreams. I want to smell your body's perfume in my bed, and taste your kiss on my mouth when I wake every morning. Most of all I want to be able to touch you and hold you and feel myself within you until you can't tell where I leave off and you begin. I want to become so much a part of your life that it would be impossible for you to separate me from you without amputating a vital part of yourself. I want your love, Maggy, not just your physical love, but all the love you have to give, and nothing less will do." He drew a shaky breath and moved away from her. "I'm very much afraid I'm wishing for something I'll never be able to have." He lowered his voice and began repacking their scattered possessions. "Not after today."

Shaken by the intensity of his declaration and frightened by his unexpected withdrawal, she sought to bring him back to her. "I *will* forgive you, even if I do get seasick and wet and embarrassed, et cetera, today. No class three section of water is going to keep me from—from feeling about you the way that I do." She inhaled deeply and cannonballed her way through the remnants of the emotional wall she'd erected out of insecurity and pain. "Nothing's going to keep me from loving you, Joshua. I *do* love you. All of the things you say you want, well, I want them too."

He stared at her with an intensity that brought a chill to her spine. "Never promise what you can't deliver, Maggy."

She answered his bold warning with a promise felt but heretofore unspoken. "Before you came into my life I couldn't let myself care for anyone. I couldn't let myself trust anyone. I wouldn't feel. I was too afraid of loving and losing again to try to reach out at all. You've changed all that. As long as you don't drown me on this roller coaster of a raft ride, I promise to love you for the rest of my life."

He cradled her close, wrapping her in a wet picnic blanket, smashed Greek olives, French bread crumbs, and his love. "I'm going to ask Deirdre to draw up an ironclad contract to that effect as soon as we get back. It's not a promise I want you to renege on later, after you're wet, seasick, and not in such a generously satisfied frame of mind."

Ten

"That was wild!"

"Imagine how thrilling a two-day trip would be!"

"Wasn't that just the greatest experience in your entire life?"

"I thought it was going to be the *final* experience of my life a couple of times."

A bevy of weary but exhilarated rafters skipped and hopped and in some cases limped their way from the landing dock up the stairs leading to the lodge, all talking at once to her and Joshua and each other and anyone else within a two-mile radius whose windows were open to hear the din.

"I'll take care of the raft and restocking supplies if you'll take our water babies inside," Joshua said to Magdelena, matching his long-legged stride to hers. "I've had about as much cheerful chattering as I can handle for one day," he added under his breath.

"I'll take them up and point them in the direction of the dining room," she promised. Anything to get away from bobbing boats and churning water. "But you're going to have to eat after-rafting snacks with them."

"Come on, Maggy." He grimaced. "You fed me enough picnic lunch to keep me alive for weeks."

"Tough. That's what happens when you eat what was supposed to be a two-person picnic lunch all by yourself with only a little help from me. Besides, someone has to preside over the table, and if you think so much as a cracker is going to stay down on my stomach . . ."

"You are a little green." He reached over to touch her, a gesture he'd repeated often on the raft. Reassuring, calming, caring.

She moved closer to the contact, some of the queasiness fading. He was good for her. "So I've been told . . . several times. They thought it was a reflection from the water."

"Chin up. It's almost over and you did amazingly well." Walking backwards, his eyes still caressing her warmly, he pressed two fingers to his lips and blew her a kiss. "Remember, I love you."

"How'd the trip go, trouble bird?" Bailey said when he met her at the door. He walked with her as she ushered the still enthusiastically talking group into the dining room where the chef had prepared a cold buffet. "Or do I even have to ask? They're walking on air. And you—did you find your water wings?"

She grimaced and turned away from the food. "Let's just say I'm still more chicken than duck, Bailey, and leave it at that."

"You're the boss. Say, why don't you find a place to roost over there and I'll fill your plate?"

She looked askance at him. "Why are you being so nice to me? And please, if you're determined to fill anyone's plate, make it your own, because I'm not getting near anything heavier than a tall glass of Alka-Seltzer and another tablet of Dramamine. I think